Happy Reading!

Victoria

Fire & Ice

VICTORIA R. MAYBURY

Halo
PUBLISHING
INTERNATIONAL

ISBN: 978-1-61244-734-6
Library of Congress Control Number: 2019904148

Printed in the United States of America

Halo Publishing International
1100 NW Loop 410
Suite 700 - 176
San Antonio, Texas 78213
www.halopublishing.com
contact@halopublishing.com

I dedicate this book to my mom and dad, who taught me everything I know about writing and storytelling, and showed me what true love looks like.

Contents

Prologue

It was a pleasant and sunny day but that did nothing to change the mood of the man waiting at a spring in the middle of a forest. He was well-built and wearing regular clothes for his status. He was dreadfully handsome and was from old money. However, no woman ever courted him for long, due to his behaviour. For, although he was handsome and rich, his heart was full of cruelty and wickedness. His shuttered eyes burned through the land surrounding him—a very pleasant, but archaic, forest with an unnatural amount of sunlight, despite the fact that the canopy was composed of ample cedar, chestnut, and dogwood trees. There was enough light to allow for the growth of wonderful, flowering bushes on the moist and fertile ground, which also housed many animals, both predator and prey.

I will make a house here, thought the man as his gaze swept around. He looked at his pocket watch again and huffed, being agitated. He still had five more minutes before the meeting with this "Creator" who had sent a messenger to him the day before. He smiled, remembering that moment.

It had been a darker day and he was in a mood that fit the day. His servants and guards knew better than to bother him, as did his few friends, who were still feeling the effects of the party the night before. By the mid-morning he was bored and agitated. Right before he was going to call his butler to bring him some bloody, violent entertainment, such as he enjoyed, he heard a tentative knock at the gilded, hardwood door that opened into his dark study.

"Come in," he had bellowed as the door slowly opened to present the housekeeper.

She looked around hesitantly, as if expecting one of the suits of armour to come alive and cleave off her head. She curtsied and said, "There is a messenger from a king at the door, Sire."

This piqued the man's interest. As he studied his impeccable nails, pretending to look for a spot of dirt on them, he queried, "Which king?"

The housekeeper curtsied and began to shake as she responded, "I don't know, Sire! He only said that this king is one you would want to obey."

The man huffed and went quiet for a few minutes, toying with his housekeeper's fear of being punished. Then he snapped his fingers and demanded that the messenger come in. The housekeeper ran out and quickly brought the messenger; a common-looking fellow in pants and shirt with a vest over the top. Such clothes looked very plain and simple in contrast to the Master of the House's furred jacket with tailored sleeves that covered a refined shirt. They were tied with a lightly-decorated belt that indicated that the master was probably a warrior. His pants were not decorated but were made from a rich fabric, and his boots were Mirage Couture boots, made from a magical leather that made them waterproof and weatherproof.

The messenger seemed unfazed by the differences between their appearances and opened his mouth to deliver the message. "The Creator, who is my Lord and King, demands you to meet him tomorrow at the spring in the Frothy Basin at the sun's zenith," spoke the messenger.

The man, angered that a person of an entirely different status would dare to speak to him like that, asked, "And if I refuse to come?"

The messenger met the man's burning gaze with sorrowful eyes. "Then," he began, "you will meet an unfortunate end, with no one to ever cherish your memory."

The man was surprisingly shaken at this thought and, after the messenger was sufficiently beaten, he released him to go back to wherever he had come from. He then went back to his study and planned his trip for the next day.

The man scowled as he remembered the messenger's words. *Who was he to talk to me like that? Doesn't he know who I am and my power over the kings in the area? There isn't anything that could destroy me or even fight one of my many army garrisons.*

The man looked at his watch again and saw that it was noon. He looked around but there wasn't anybody coming. Then he felt it! It was a powerful quiet, profoundly different from the quiet before. Now there was no wind, no animal sounds. It was as if everything had died. He gripped his sword buckled at his side. Although it was beautiful, now was not the time to study the merits or appearance of the sword! He looked around again, this time with a heaviness in the pit of his stomach that surprised him. He hadn't felt such nervousness in the last five of his twenty years.

There was a sound like a crack of thunder to his right and he jumped, looking in that direction. "Who's there? I demand you answer!" he yelled in the direction from which the noise had come.

There was no answer.

Suddenly, he was enveloped in a dark, swirling cloud, with light streaming from the top. The light was blinding as much as the darkness was suffocating, but the man stubbornly tried to look at the light.

As he finally dropped his gaze from the burning light, a mighty voice, which made the thunder before sound like a little child's clap, spoke. "Why do you ignore my commands, and beat my servants, Archer? Your wickedness has become so great that I should wipe you from the face of this world! You think only of what you want to do and have no love for others. Instead, you only bring misery and death to all."

Archer, hearing these words, was enraged and shouted, "Who are you? I don't have to take orders from you or anyone! I am my own person and I do what I want when I want. Who are you, that I should care what you say?"

The voice boomed, "I am your King! I made you and this world. I was never born nor can I die, for I am forever."

"So what? You claim to be a god? I don't believe in the gods!" replied Archer, becoming more and more furious.

The voice boomed again, "It doesn't matter whether you believe in a god, I am real. And I have come to punish you, and wipe the very essence of you from this world."

When Archer heard this, he began to shake, being overcome with fear for himself. "No! Please don't! I'll do anything to live! Anything! Please, whoever you are, let me live!" he begged the light from whence the voice was emanating. "Have mercy!"

There was silence and some of the tendrils of the dark cloud began to crawl to him. The voice returned and cursed him. "From this day on, you are frozen at this age. So you shall remain until you both find and understand love, and as well as relinquish control over your own life. For there is one who is worse than you. I will charge you to destroy him. However, the time for his destruction has not come yet. When it comes, you will find joy but also sorrow."

The light pulsed a few times, each pulse brighter and stronger. As Archer watched, transfixed, the light then vanished. The cloud of darkness then crashed upon Archer, plummeting him into a thick and tangible black sleep.

When Archer woke up, he found he was sore. He started to stiffly stand, but every muscle in his body burned as he did so. He looked around at his surroundings, while also dusting off his now ripped and ragged clothes. The fields of dust and sand stretched to the horizon, only broken by the darkness of the clouds above and the rock before him. He stepped back, surprised at what had happened to the Frothy Basin. Everything had been replaced by desert. Even the spring from the rock had dried up.

He looked to the sky and spoke, "I will do as you have spoken."

Archer left, going back to his castle, determined to forget about what had happened, but also promising to act better and show love to all.

* * * * * *

In another part of the old Frothy Basin, another man, also cursed, woke up to a similar surrounding. He shook his dirty fist at the sky. "I will find you!" he promised, his green eyes flashing. "I will kill all those who believe in you and lastly I will kill you!"

A voice boomed back, "This place is a promise that your curse will not be broken until you do as I say. I can keep my promise, can you?"

The man was enraged at the voice and walked away on a crooked and winding path back to civilization, determined to keep his promise and show whoever or whatever that voice was who was boss.

CACOETHES

200 years later

It was another bright and pleasant day, and yet the mood was sombre despite the many voices that tittered happily in the Cartier Castle. The castle was very old and had not been overtaken for many centuries. It was maintained very well, and its many well-washed windows were in perfect condition. It was through one of these windows that a young woman was staring from her bedroom into the fields beyond the black onyx walls. The young woman normally hated black, but today it felt right that the walls were weeping with her. Her hair was in a shaggy double braid that she had slept in. She pulled on it with a scorched and scarred hand while she gazed at the sky. She was hoping He would heed her silent prayer for peace and protection as she entered a new and unwanted phase in her life. Her name was Ash Cartier, and it wasn't the first time she wished that she wasn't the daughter of a wealthy and important chieftain in Dasica. Her country promoted itself as a place of peace and prosperity, but Ash knew better.

When she was younger, she had accompanied her mother to a local market to look at unnecessary baubles that her mother, Marie, wanted for a festival. Her mother had found some strange pin that "talked to her," as she would always say when she wanted something. While waiting for her, Ash had gone exploring and had met an old man with a face that spoke of many happy times as well as of hard times.

He had looked at her with a twinkle in his green eyes. "Do you want to hear something beautiful, little one?" he had asked her. A sweet smile had crossed his face, showing a mouth of clean teeth, although a few were missing.

She had nodded and he had told her of a man who was not just a man but who had loved everyone in the world. This man had wanted to save them from what was to come so he had died to protect them. The man's green eyes had moistened as he told this story, making Ash think it was more than a fictional tale.

At the end of the story, Ash had asked if they were safe because of what this man, named Joshua, had done. The man had shaken his head sadly and replied that there was something that they had to do if they wanted to be safe forever. He had said that they had to relinquish their control over their lives and become part of His family. Confused, Ash had questioned how they could be part of a dead man's family, but the old man had smiled and tapped her head, praising her as a thinker. He then had explained that even though Joshua had been a man, he was also something else. The man then had looked around them to see if anyone was listening and pulled Ash close enough to whisper in her ear that Joshua is also the Creator!

Ash had sucked in a breath. Even though she had only been five years old at the time, she knew that talking about gods could get you into serious trouble, and could even be viewed as treason against the leaders, because it affirmed that they weren't in total control.

The man had slipped a giant book into her small hands, telling her to read it in order to learn more about Joshua. He also had warned her to not show anyone the Book. She had nodded and had just hidden the Book when her mother had called for her. (After Ash's departure, her mother had bought three other pins aside from the first one that had "spoken to her.") The man had grabbed her arm as she turned and had told her to find him if she ever wanted to talk more about the story.

She had nodded again and run to where her mother was standing, looking for her. Marie admonished Ash not to wander off and they soon had returned home to the twelve-towered castle. Once there, Ash had run to her room and locked the door, in order to start reading the interesting book in safety.

From that book, she learned about how the world came to exist, and much more. It had taken her an entire month of reading to go through it one time. Not satisfied with that, she continued to read it over and over, sprawled on her bed, trying to understand the Creator better. As she learned more and grew up, Ash continued to meet with and talk to the old man as much as possible.

Ash looked at the bed and smiled seeing the indent of where she had always sprawled to read the Book. Then her smile faltered as her blue eyes turned to look at her hands covered in white, luminescent scars. They were slightly lighter than her already-fair skin. She had gotten the scars from being burned, as a punishment for disobeying her father. Her eyes released a few rivulets of water that she let drip down her face. There was a knock at her door, and she looked at the clock on her wall above the writing desk. It was time. She sighed and straightened up. She was nineteen, not six, and slouching would not be acceptable.

"Come in, please," she said in her soft, lilting Glaydin accent, mimicking how a lady should speak, or at least as her mother said ladies should speak. Since the royal court was situated far away in the capital of Dasica, Ash had never actually heard someone from the court speak.

Ash was not surprised when her mother came in with her three ladies' maids. However, she was surprised to see Carmel Baum, the woman who had been her trainer until the day before, as well. Her old trainer smiled at her gently. "Gillith Preslar sends his condolences for not being able to come to the wedding today, but wishes you all happiness on your special day," Carmel informed Ash in her thick eastern accent.

Tears of fear and anguish pricked Ash's eyes, but she nodded to Carmel. She met her trainer's red eyes in the mirror while the maids took off her shift and began to usher her to the steaming tub of water with essential oils to cleanse her. The trainer clapped her hand on Ash's now-bare shoulder and left. Ash smiled, feeling some warmth enter her. That small action held more meaning than anything the old fighter could have said, which wasn't surprising since Carmel had been hired for her fighting ability, not for her way with words. Ash realized that she was much like that, even though she had a fiery temper that needed to be constantly reined in.

Ash finally focused on her mother, who was delivering commands to the maids at a rapid pace. Marie wore a dress that left her shoulders uncovered, with the straps hanging just off the shoulders very fashionably. The bodice hugged her mother's tall, but slim, body and puffed out into a ballroom-like skirt that fell almost to the floor. The dress was a green velvet with silver thread that matched her short bob and which was woven into the material in order to create fancy designs that meant absolutely nothing. Marie also wore a tripled-tiered necklace with jade beads and figurines, as well as a matching brooch, earrings, and hair comb. Ash rolled her eyes at the excessive nature of her mother, which she had never understood. The maids were also wearing their special clothes under protective white aprons.

"I guess everyone is waiting on me to get clothed and be led to the slaughter," grumbled Ash.

Her mother's dark brown eyes shot toward her. "Do not say such things, child! You should be happy. This is your wedding day. At least pretend to be," said Marie, her dark eyes twinkling with something akin to joy.

Ash met her gaze as the maids finished cleaning her from head to toe. "I'll pretend to enjoy it as much as you pretend to care for me," she replied, her anger unleashing slightly. "If you did care, you wouldn't have encouraged Father to accept this horrid man's proposal. You simply want to get rid of your embarrassing daughter who believes in such treasonous thoughts. So, what better way of accomplishing that than by throwing her into the hands of a man who is loyal only to himself?"

Marie's eyes flashed dangerously, and the maids paused nervously before continuing their work. "First, you have never met him. However, it is true that I would rather die than spend another day knowing you believe in such stupidity! Third, you were never a lady! You would rather learn about swordsmanship than the rules of court. You are too reckless, Ash, and I will not have you in this house. So, yes, I helped encourage your father to ally with the most powerful man on this side of the mountains. Trading you for substances we needed was an easy decision to make," admitted Marie as she swept out of the room. "Make sure she's ready!" was all she said, and then she was gone.

Ash's jaw dropped. She knew this was a political alliance and a way to silence her, but she didn't know she was being sold! The maids dried her off and added creams and lotions to her skin in order to cover her scars for the day. Then Ash finally spotted the dress, and her heart sank. It was a monstrosity of white satin and tulle! She didn't mind dresses and liked to look nice, but this dress was floor-length and filled with little fancy baubles that could pay off all the debts that the Cartier family had! More than that, it looked like a prison, to keep Ash from trying to escape.

She sent up a quick prayer for guidance as the maids applied makeup to her naked body. It was a vain attempt to cover the rest of the scars from the accidents during training under Carmel, as well as from other times. The maids then put her in the three pairs of underclothes, and, lastly, the dress. They finished the fine makeup work last of all. When they were finally done, the maids ushered her to the floor-length mirror, where she finally got to see herself. Ash gasped at what she saw. Though the dress was huge, it made her look like a princess, and the makeup made her blue eyes look like burning spheres. Her hair was kept down but had a braided crown with small blue flowers woven in.

Ash turned to the maids, who were beaming. "Thank you!" she said as she took their hands. "You did a wonderful job, and I will pray for you when I go to my new house."

The maids smiled and nodded, quickly filing out of the room; the last one wiping her eyes a bit. Ash smiled. She was going to miss them, even though they didn't believe what she did. They were kind, but distant, as if she would infect them with treasonous thoughts. Ash knew she could not do so, but everyone seemed to fear that she would.

She stared at her room and then glanced out the door to see if anyone was coming. For once, the ornate hallway was silent. She crossed to her desk and took out of a secret compartment the Book the old man had given her so long ago. She slipped it into a hidden pocket and turned as she heard muffled footsteps coming down the hall. A few moments later, her father, Lucas Cartier III, appeared in her doorway. She resembled her dad more than she did her mother. She had her father's brown hair, though his hair had turned fully silver now, along with same fair skin and tall build. Her stubbornness came from her mother, but that was about it. Her father also had a burn scar that ran from the left side of his forehead to his left nostril, and they shared the same energetic blue eyes. Ash looked into her father's eyes now and saw a look that she had only seen once before: pity. It chilled her to the bone, and she took a slight step back to gather her thankfully-plain-white gloves. She met his gaze once again, and Lucas nodded. It was time.

Their walk through the old castle to the throne room was oddly comforting to Ash. She had walked through these halls many times, normally so quietly that she was like a shadow, which gave her the title "Shadowwalker" in warrior circles. Unfortunately, she wasn't a warrior now, but rather a mess being handed over to someone who could "clean her up." Ash shuddered at the thoughts those words brought her, but she knew there was nothing she could do. She had to honour her family's wishes and pray that she could hold on to what she knew to be right. Soon they were at the large double doors of the throne room and she could hear the music swelling. In a few seconds, her father would escort her into the hands of her new husband. Her stomach twisted at the thought of being with that man, and even though she hadn't heard much about him, what she had heard made her nervousness skyrocket. She inhaled and exhaled slowly, trying to rid herself of the feeling, and prayed for the third time that day for guidance and safety. Her stomach settled slightly. The heavy doors were open, and the one who was supposed to care for and protect her led her like a lamb to the slaughter.

Ash looked at the throne room. She had been in here many times but every time it amazed her, and this time it was decorated for the occasion. There were lustrous braziers that circled the sixteen columns and cast a golden light on the walls of the room, which was decorated with garlands of lilacs and lilies. A sanguine rug ran down the centre of the room to the doors, splitting the round room in half, with long wooden benches on either side of it. There was a chestnut throne at the front of the room but it was not in use that day.

The rug seemed endless as Ash and her father slowly walked down it. Ash turned and looked at the ceiling, where there was a small skylight that was surrounded by legends and stories telling the Cartier history. Ash finally looked at the people on the raised dais. There was Adam Firedraft at the front: the head elder under her father, the chieftain. He had brown dreadlocks that always fell over his full-but-charming face. He had brown, almost black, eyes that were set far back in his head, making him seem like a snake. He stood a head shorter than the man beside him.

Ash turned her gaze toward the man who she was to call husband and saw shuttered brown eyes that gave her an icy chill. He possessed caramel skin and long, wavy, brown hair that was tied with a simple, black-leather tie. He was half a head taller than her and wore a black suit with a white vest and blue cravat for the occasion. He did not look like the monster that she had imagined, but rather like a man who simply wanted to finish the deal and leave.

Behind him were three people—guards, most likely, due to the fact that they were bristling with weaponry. First, there was a man taller than her almost-husband, with shaggy but well-groomed golden hair and a half-feral face. His golden eyes resembled a griffin's as they watch their prey, and he stood with the grace of one who understands power. The lady behind him was at the opposite end of the spectrum. She had wavy, green hair that fell into a low bun, with a few strands framing her naturally cheerful face. She was quite short compared to her companion, with the top of her head only reaching his shoulder. Ash wondered if she was a half-elf, but her eyes gave away that she was a full elf, due to them being a violet colour. She winked at Ash and gave her a smile, which buoyed her spirit slightly. Given the situation, Ash responded with a slight smile and looked to see the man beyond her. He had silver hair that had nothing to do with his age and had a set of piercing amber eyes that made him seem insightful as he continued to gaze around the room. He was closer to the height of the golden-haired one than the girl but looked to be just as deadly as the other two. All three were dressed in black clothing with cravats, or a sash in the girl's case, that matched the groom's clothing.

Finally, Ash and her father made it to where Elder Adam stood. Lucas smiled and nodded at the elder and proceeded to place his daughter's gloved hands into her future husband's. Lucas went and sat with his wife, and the ceremony began. It started with the story of how George Cartier I had chosen his bride by lining up all the village women and choosing the one who was the most gentle. This story Ash knew by heart because it had always been told at any event that she had ever gone to. George had decreed that every child in the Cartier line must be wed in the throne room, whether male or female. Ash wished that he had decreed that they must consent to the marriage, but it seemed like the days of chivalry were a thing of the past. She focused on her breathing, and the elder's droning became background noise.

She almost missed it when he asked her the only question in the entire ceremony that she had to answer. "Ash 'Shadowwalker' Cartier, will you promise to care for Fross 'Slayer' Arcop for as long as you have breath?"

She sucked in a quiet breath and looked up from where her gaze had been burning a hole into the floor, and looked at the elder and then at Fross. *Fross is a stupid name*, she thought. When she met his gaze, he raised his eyebrows, looking slightly perplexed at her hesitation, and she realized that this man should be approached with care. Keeping her gaze there, she began to answer the elder, but just as she opened her mouth there was a loud, resounding crash, followed by the sound of an explosion.

The throne room shook and was filled with smoke, dust, and the screams of people. Ash was roughly handed off by someone and dragged through the mess.

There were the sounds of gunshots and of swords cutting people down as Ash was taken away. By the time she saw who had grabbed her, they were almost to her room. The green-haired lady pushed her into her room and locked the door, not saying a word, and ran away, the carpet muffling her footsteps.

Ash was in shock. *Who would want to ruin the wedding?* she wondered as she started to react. She slipped out of her dress and threw the Book and a few other items into a knapsack that she tied to her waist, on top of the pants and long-sleeved shirt that she had thrown on. They were mismatched, but at that moment Ash didn't care. She was getting out, and fast! Then she tied her bedsheets together to form a makeshift rope, tied the rope to a bedpost, and stepped out of the window. She quickly scaled down the tower and was able to jump to the outer black wall and slide down into a grassy plain.

Ash was free. She quickly walked away, pulling her hood and scarf up over the masterpiece that the maids had done. *They are probably dead now.* The thought popped into her head and she quickly shoved it away. Ash had to stay free. She could mourn the dead later. They probably were dead even if Ash didn't want to accept that just yet. Her father had always been light on guards and warriors due to the fact that they would like to get paid for their work. So they had only had four guards, Carmel Baum, and a young warrior, Gillith Preslar, who had become Ash's best—and only—friend. She and Gill had grown up together under Carmel's training, and he was like a brother to her.

Now she worried about him. *If he comes back, what will he do? Should I leave a message for him or just pray that he finds his way?* She decided to go to the old hunting house, which she knew was nearby, and, hopefully, he would figure out where she was. She smiled a real smile for the first time that day and slowed down a bit to enjoy her newfound freedom, even though it had come at a terrible cost.

Then there was a shout. "Hey, you! Come back to your wedding!" a rough, male voice shouted.

Ash froze. *Was she caught? How had they found her?* Then she looked at her hands and saw that she still wore the gloves. She chided herself for her stupidity and bolted into the woods. As she reached the entrance to the forest, an ironic thought popped into her head: *She was now being in hunted in the woods where she had once been a hunter.*

FERLY

Ash doubled over, panting. She had been running for hours and had finally lost the people on her trail. From the sounds of it, she wasn't the only one who was tired. She paused and leaned back on a tree and looked up at the forest canopy. The forest was dead silent. The sunlight danced cheerfully in dappled patches on the floor. Ash looked around, trying to get her bearings, though she was terrible with directions. She decided to move forward and go from there. She took out her blade and tied it to her thigh. The blade was a small, thin, jagged bit of silver with a grip wrapped in a rare, red-salmon leather. It had a razor-sharp point, so if she was fast enough she could poke her enemies full of holes before they could get in a swing. The blade had a curled crossguard that provided Ash protection from incoming attacks; the pommel had the Cartier crest on it, which depicted twelve towers.

Ash picked her way through the forest's undergrowth with the silence of a shadow and the speed of a bird. Had she had time to enjoy the forest she would have noticed the scents from the flowers finally blossoming from the winter's harsh grip. Spring had finally come to Dasica and, unlike other countries, the spring was normally very dry while all the rain came in the summer.

Ash stopped and looked around deciding which way to go, again wishing Gill was there to help her. She remembered a time when she was twelve years old and Gill was fifteen. She had run too far from the castle and into the woods, following a white rabbit, with Gill trailing her until he had lost her. Finally, the rabbit had run into a hole and she had looked up and seen that she was in an unknown part of the forest. She panicked and began to run here and there trying to find the way back. She couldn't remember anything that she saw and broke down on the ground, praying for the Creator to help her, and curled up in a ball, crying. Gill found her within an hour and had picked her up, even though they were the same height, and carried her home. She woke up in his arms and looked at his amber eyes that were etched with concern. Once he saw that she was awake, he had stopped walking, hugged her, and said for her to never run away alone again. Ash smiled at the memory. *Now Gill, here I am running away alone, please find me.* Though Ash had been trained as a warrior and could hold her own in a fight, Gill always had that little extra on her. He had been able to master all methods of fighting and had more experience than her, going on the few missions that her father had ever ordered.

Caught up in her memories, she didn't hear the slight crackling of the undergrowth until it was too late. A burst of pain in her left arm brought her back to reality. She yelped and looked to see a short arrow lodged in her arm. Ash ran through the forest, swerving side-to-side much like a rabbit does, until the throbbing and sudden dizziness forced her to stop or drop. She hid behind a tree and another arrow shot past her. The throbbing was too much to keep running. Ash knew she had to hide or to stand her ground. She looked at the oak that she was behind and made the decision. She jumped and grabbed the branch, much as she had done as a child, with both arms. That was a mistake and it cost her. She fell to the mossy ground with a thump, bringing her killers' attention if they didn't already know where she was. Turning to the arrow, she broke the protruding piece off, holding it by the fletching. *If she was going to go down, she would go down fighting.*

The archer came into view first, not doing a good job in covering her tracks. The plain leather braid in her blue hair marked her like a sword—or, in this case, like a bow—for hire. Ash threw the rock that she had picked up in the bushes away from her and the archer moved toward that sound with her back to Ash, who crept up quietly and took the girl's knife. It was a small throwing knife by the looks of it, not more dangerous than the bow in the girl's hands. Ash stood up and quickly put the girl in a chokehold, knocking down her bow in the process. The smaller girl struggled and got Ash with a quick and disorienting headbutt. Already dizzy, Ash released her hold on the girl and took several steps back as her vision swam. Ash sank to the ground just in time as another arrow struck the tree behind her, embedding itself where Ash's body had been seconds before. Enraged, Ash rushed the girl, who had reached for her knife and realized it wasn't there. Tackling the sellsword, Ash pinned the girl on the ground, trying to cut off her circulation. The girl twisted out of her grasp and rammed her left arm. Ash screamed—a sound of blood and fury—and brought out the throwing knife. She lifted it to stab the girl's heart, but then thought about what the Creator would have her do and brought the hilt down on the girl's head, knocking her out with a loud *thwack*. Ash put the blade away and rested her hands on her pants and grimaced. She disliked the feeling of killing, though she knew there were many who did enjoy the gruesome act. It was wrong to kill, even as the last of her family. It wasn't okay to kill those who had murdered the Cartiers, even if it was a law of the land: Revenge Law.

There was a crash through the trees and two more sellswords burst into view, with red spray staining their rugged faces and coating their leather armour. The one who, by the looks of his earring, was their leader spotted the still form of their companion and looked toward Ash.

"You killed her!" he snarled in a very guttural accent, his teeth white against his dark skin. He brought up his simple red stained broadsword and pointed it in Ash's direction. "Now you will die!"

Ash brought out both knives in preparation for the fight and kept both men in view, knowing that this was not the time to fight fair. The leader charged her, swinging his broadsword. She ducked it and lunged to stab his stomach, but misjudged the distance was only able to scratch it. The man, now fueled by a blood rage, jabbed her thigh with the point of the sword, driving it deep into her leg and making her leg crumple beneath her. Ash screamed as the pain washed over her, dulling her senses. As the man swung to decapitate her, she rolled out of the way and into the legs of the last sellsword. She stabbed just under his kneecap, crippling his leg. The man fell to the ground, crying out, and landed a blow to her eye with his fist. She retaliated and kicked him with her sturdy boot in his stomach as she struggled to her feet. He went unconscious with a slight grunt and she turned around to face the last man, who had frozen for a second but was now coming at her again. She aimed and threw the archer's knife and hit him just below the collarbone. It slowed him down but did not stop him. He came at her, pulling the knife out, ready to use it. She grabbed the only thing left in her arsenal of weapons, the butt of the arrow, and jumped to him. The man knocked her away with the flat of the sword, apparently wanting to make her death slow and painful. He pinned her under his boot and bent down.

"Looks like the last little Cartier is stuck in the mud," he tsked mockingly. "Someone should have told you not to play in the woods."

She mumbled something, and he bent to hear it, slowly increasing the pressure on her chest.

"What was that?" he asked, getting close to her face.

"At least I won't die in these woods," Ash replied and then stabbed him in the eye. She kicked him in the stomach with her undamaged leg. He pulled away and collapsed beside her, growing still within a few breaths.

Ash got up, wincing, and supported herself against a tree. If she was dizzy with just the arrow wound, the world was now spinning in circles. She slowly collected her weapons, not bothering to clean them, and staggered off toward the sound of water.

She had made it to what looked like a small stream of fresh water when a rich voice sounded behind her.

"There you are!"

Ash turned, almost falling, hoping the voice to be Gill's. It wasn't, but rather it belonged to the man with the golden hair who had been behind Fross that morning. He was dressed in the same clothes, but now with a small cut high on his cheek, below his left eye. He began to approach her carefully, as one approaches a wild beast. Given her appearance, that wasn't much of a surprise. She backed away slowly, trying not to fall but wavering from time to time, and brought out her dagger.

"Stay away!" she shouted and gestured with the blade. "I'm not afraid to use this!"

"Come, come, child, don't hurt yourself with that weapon," he said with a smirk on his face.

The words enraged Ash and she ran uncaring, full tilt into the man, who evaded her disoriented strike, grabbed her shoulder, and flipped her onto her back. The wind was knocked out of her but she continued to fight as best she could. Not because she was stubborn but because she feared what would happen if he took her. *Are they going to execute me like the rest of my family, or are they going to do something worse?* The man slowly but surely pinned each of her legs with his own and grabbed a harsh-smelling cloth and planted it on her mouth and nose. Ash slowed down as her vision tunnelled and everything went black. The man picked her up like one does a bride and carried her to a helicopter in a nearby clearing.

Haon Pridegazer, a half-elf with vibrant green hair, pink eyes, and a slight frame for a guard, was in the pilot seat. His fellow guard Onul Jebel, a changeling whose vibrant red hair and green eyes looked large in a face full of sharp angles, was sitting beside him. They looked up as Ash, limp in the man's arms, came into view. Onul jumped out of the helicopter and helped the golden-haired man get Ash settled. The golden-haired man took Onul's place by Haon so that Onul could use her field medicine and gifts to keep the blood at bay in Ash's injured body.

"Fross isn't going to like this, Alaistair," she murmured to him.

"Fross doesn't like much," replied Alaistair curtly, taking his place by the pilot. "She is the only hope we have, though."

He made a sign to Haon and they took off.

******

Ash groaned. It felt as if a hellhound had used her as a chew toy and then trampled her. Everything ached, especially her head. It was like a bomb had gone off inside of it and no one could relieve the pressure. In all her years of training, she had never felt this bad before. Her hand touched someone's skin and she pulled back and forced her eyes open. There was a man before her, gazing at her with cold, mismatched eyes—one brown and one green. He looked her up and down. It seemed that he knew she would live, despite the thin healer's sheet that someone had placed over her.

"Well, Mrs. Arcop, it looks like you might survive us yet," her almost-husband said in a melodic accent, with the slightest bit of humour touching his tone and face.

"Don't call me that, the wedding was interrupted," Ash ground out through the pain of working her jaw. That punch had really done a number on her.

"All right, Shadowwalker, I will send you off to the healer to finish what Onul started," he said in a frosty voice.

She didn't know who Onul was, but she didn't like this one bit. She was rolled away by someone, into a room just down the hall from where she had been. As she left, Ash heard voices raised in a heated conversation.

"I thought I made it clear that we have no-abduction policy, Alaistair!" The melodic voice had been replaced by an ice-cold one.

"She wasn't cooperating! What did you expect me to do, Fross?" The rich-voiced Alaistair replied unconcernedly to the cold menace in Fross's voice.

"Maybe not flip her on her back and drug her like a common criminal! She's my wife!" Fross yelled.

"Well, she was also bleeding out and feral with fear. I did what I had to so that she could get medical attention. You know that, Fross. Just as you know she didn't want to marry you, nor is she your wife." Alaistair's voice softened. "We both know she is the one."

And with that, Ash lost touch with the world and was greeted again by the darkness of unconsciousness.

AUBADE

It was sunny when Ash opened her eyes. She was standing in a field outside of her home. The sky was a pretty blue and everything looked perfect. She looked toward the forest and felt a strange pull toward it. *What's this?* Unable to stop her feet from moving forward, Ash followed the magnetic pull, brimming with curiosity. The ground began to roll underneath Ash and she was thrown to the ground as the green grass became gravel. She looked up and the sky had become red with fire and there was a castle in the distance. As Ash stood up, the sky began to rain fire and rock that exploded into puffs of noxious gas. She ran for the stone castle and, as she drew near, one of the heavy metal doors swung open and a tall, dark man gestured for her to speed up. He was yelling something at her as well, but she couldn't understand him due to the explosions that surrounded her. She hit the drawbridge in a dead run, keeping her feet even as the bridge began to crumble into dust. Ash jumped for the door and felt a moment of weightlessness and dread in the pit of her stomach. The man grabbed her arm and swung her into the castle. She stumbled and rolled, to release the momentum from the throw, and then got up only to see that the scenery had changed once again. It was her wedding day and she was standing, holding hands with her husband, as was the custom. Looking up she was greeted with hooded green eyes and soft, ash-blond curls that framed a wild face. She looked to the elder standing behind them, who smiled as he bled out. Horror filled her as the man to whom she had looked up fell at her feet, his blood pooling outward. Ash ripped her gaze from the still body of Adam Firedraft and looked to the congregation. The throne room disappeared and in its place were the bodies of the people with whom she had grown up, being set on fire. There was a blood trail leading back to her and ending with an arrow at her feet. Ash gasped, trying to keep down her breakfast. Something grabbed her ankle, making her jump. Looking down, Ash saw her mother, gasping for breath.

"You did this," she hissed at her daughter as her spirit left her.

Ash backed up and ran into someone. Turning, she saw the tall man and his green eyes. He smiled gently, so out of place for the carnage around him, and stroked Ash's chin.

"I'll come for you, my lovely," he purred into her ear.

Ash's insides tightened as the world swam in front of her.

* * * * * *

She bolted up violently in bed and looked around at her surroundings, again feral with fear. Slowly, as the memories of her wedding day came back to her, Ash's heart began to crumble into itself. But before she could fall apart, a blinding light filled the room. She squinted at the light but began to relax as a familiar and comforting voice spoke.

"You have done well, my child," said the Creator in His booming voice that marked this interaction as a vision. "You obeyed your parents' wishes even though they were not your own. But be warned that the path from here is not an easy one."

Ash's breath caught in her throat as she waited for the Creator to explain what He meant. The golden light swirled.

The voice softened as the Creator ended, "You must keep your wits about you and keep my words close to your heart. You will meet many people, but remember that their true self is seen in their heart and not in outward appearance. Be strong, have courage, and know that I am with you."

Still sitting in bed, Ash bowed her head and replied.

"I live to serve you, my King and Creator."

And with that, the light vanished and Ash sunk into the familiar post-vision darkness.

* * * * * *

As Ash slowly dragged herself from the confines of her deep and murky sleep, she heard the murmurs of voices. As she walked the line between sleep and wakefulness, the voices separated into distinct male and female voices.

"Chester!" the husky female voice exclaimed. "She is coming around."

"Ok, Blanche." A steady male voice instructed, "Fetch her a glass of water and some of the ketacept for her pain. She will definitely be feeling some after going against Alaistair."

Ash sensed movement and opened her eyes to see a middle-aged man, with bulging hazel eyes and blond locks pulled back from his face, staring at her with open concern. There was a clatter of footsteps and a slightly younger woman stepped into Ash's field of vision. She was a plumper woman than some, with pink layered hair kept in a bun at the back of her head and affectionate violet eyes that betrayed her elf heritage. Both were wearing white, crestless aprons over their regular clothes, marking them as healers. *Was she at a hospital? Possibly, but then her belongings would have been searched. Ash's heart clenched. Had they found the Book? If they had, why wasn't she in the dungeon awaiting trial? Or were they accomplices of Fross? Did they take part in the murders?* The thoughts raced through Ash's mind as she sat up with a jerk that sent her head and thigh into a burning, throbbing spasm that threatened to pull her back to the sweetness of unconsciousness.

"Oh, dear," said the man named Chester, his voice lilting in a Werstrom speech pattern. "Blanche, you best give her the ketacept first." A small smile graced his thin lips, as if her pain was something amusing.

The lady, Blanche, bustled forward with a drink the colour of Ash's azure eyes in a small clay cup.

"Come on, drink, dear," she encouraged with an impeccable bedside manner. "It will ease the pain." Her tone was gentle like she was talking to a young child.

The tone calmed Ash slightly and she reached for the cup. She pinched her nose and swigged the concoction back and gagged immediately. The taste was putrid, like mixing salt into a glass of wine. Ash gasped and grabbed for the offered glass of water, which helped to partially rid the taste from her mouth. Chester chuckled and Ash transfixed him with her blazing stare as heat crept up her face. *He hadn't just tasted that terrible drink. What did he know?* Ash's anger rose within her and she opened her mouth.

"I suppose you find patients amusing during their times of weakness. Wait until I'm better and punch you in the mouth!"

The man just smirked at her weak threat and offered her his hand. She looked at it for a long second and then skeptically at him.

"My name is Dr. Chester Ward. You may call me Chester." He spoke with the arrogance of a healer. He gestured to the taller lady beside him, his eyes grazing affectionately over her face. "This is Blanche Todd, my assistant." He said her name with such awkwardness that Ash almost felt sorry for the healer's obvious crush on the mother hen beside him.

"Where am I?" asked Ash quickly, to end the feeling of intruding on the two of them. "Is this a public clinic?" She looked for signs of other people but found none.

"No, this is Lord Arcop's personal clinic," the assistant replied with a welcoming smile. "Only the best for his wife."

Ash shuddered at the title.

"I am not his wife," she said blandly, trying to keep down her rage.

Ash inquired further.

"So, where am I? You never answered that question." Noticing the hesitation in the healers' responses, Ash continued with a sigh. "I guess it is one of those need-to-know answers that I won't be getting an answer to soon." She settled back into the sturdy medical pillow and pulled the matching white sheets up to her chin. *What was in that drink?* She had begun to close her eyes when a familiar voice shot them back open.

"Is she awake yet?" a melodic voice, belonging to only one person she knew, asked impatiently.

"Yes, sir," the stiff voice from Chester replied.

Ash looked toward the door and saw the healers quickly departing, leaving her with the bane of her life.

He walked over to the bed with the swagger of an all-powerful man. Fross raked his gaze over her body once again and then looked into her eyes, his hair falling into his face and nearly hiding his mismatched eyes, one chocolate and the other emerald green. He shoved his hair back into place while holding her gaze. *This is ridiculous*, Ash thought.

"Why are you here?" she snapped.

His eyebrows rose and his eyes twinkled with mockery.

"Not even asking after your parents or about how long you have been out . . . interesting," he said in that sarcastic, yet melodic, voice that was getting on her nerves. "Well, since you are so interested—" he stopped as if to create suspense. "You have been unconscious for half a week. And as for why I am here: Am I not allowed to see how my bride is doing?" His eyes scanned her face, looking for any sign of emotion, while Ash kept her face devoid of such betrayal.

"We both know why you wanted to marry me, so let's drop the act." She spat the words as if they were poison. "You wanted a deal and I was the price. So, marry the girl, kill the family with sellswords while making it look like an assassination by another enemy, and inherit the supposed fortune. Then, get rid of the girl, who is more of an embarrassment than a useful tool. Not a bad plan, except for one detail: My father had no enemies or fortune. You lost money on this skirmish of yours." She ended it with a smirk, thinking that if she was going to die she might as well take him down a peg.

The result was not as she desired. Fross looked at her with cool indifference.

"If that is what you think, I will not try to dissuade you of it, but before you continue—" He leaned in close, gripping the sides of the bed to steady himself as he gazed into her eyes, the scent of his aftershave tickling her nose. "I am not an enemy you want to make."

With that, Fross left in a storm of icy rage. Ash trembled for a few moments. *What is he?* She was accustomed to the feelings that each person, human or otherwise, gave her, but Fross? Fross was a different beast altogether, and might have been an actual beast. The stories of his cruelty had reached her ears before the wedding but she had always assumed that they had been exaggerated one way or another. But now, now Ash wasn't so sure. His gaze had not been human, not fully at least. She had to find out the mysteries surrounding this place and her clan's death.

Ash yawned and tried to get comfortable on the mattress without shifting her wounded parts. A feat not always easy to complete, mind you. She finally got into a spot that felt just right and, with her conversations with the healers and Fross running through her mind, slowly fell into a dreamless sleep.

PHILOPHOBIA

Ash stretched as she yawned. It had been a week since she had been taken to Arcop Manor which, unlike the title implied, was a castle with eleven towers, grand windows, and dark red stone surrounding it, making Ash think about how much blood might have been shed here. She shuddered remembering the executions at her family's castle, tears pricking her eyes for the innocent deaths. Some of those executed had deserved their deaths due to their wicked actions, but others—those she still mourned—had been condemned and killed simply on account of their unpopular beliefs. Shaking her head to rid herself of the memories, Ash rose from her new bed and looked around her prison for the first time since being brought upstairs. It was a simple room but ever-fashionable with its dark-brown panelling and large glass doors that led out to a porch overlooking a garden. The room was equipped with a writing desk and a small sitting room beside the grand fireplace. There was an en suite bathroom, which had closet, and, of course, a bed. Ash wrapped a white dressing gown over her light sleeping shift and went to the balcony, enjoying the sunrise as it crested the mountains. She leaned on the banister and, as the sun slowly bathed the castle in a golden-red glow, she thought about what had happened after her first conversation with Fross.

Ash had woken up a few hours after having drunk the ketacept and smelled the delicious scent of food. Her stomach, betraying her, grumbled, and Ash heard a light chuckle. In walked, with a plateful of meat and greens, the green-haired she-elf who had been at the wedding.

"I thought you might be hungry," the she-elf stated, rolling the r in hungry and giving the hs a harsh sound. She set the food on a table beside the med-bed and reached for Ash, who shifted out of her reach.

Her violet eyes flashed with impatience. "I'm not going to hurt you, Shadowwalker. I'm making sure you don't hurt yourself even further." The rs were rolled once again.

Ash let the she-elf help her get into a seated position and set the food in front of her. Ash, not waiting for extra encouragement, dug into the feast, sending up a prayer of thanks as she did so. The food was gone within a few minutes and Ash wiped her hands on the napkin that had accompanied the meal. Looking up, she saw the she-elf watching her from across the room. The she-elf sent Ash another smile, like at the wedding.

"My name is Paola Lambert. Weird, right?" the she-elf said, cheerfully crossing the floor and beginning to pick up the tray, only to put it back on the bedside table. "My mother was from the south and my father, well . . ." She sat down. "My father was a warrior of royal lineage. Thus the strange name." Ash looked at the she-elf and saw amusement twinkling in her molten eyes.

"Anyway," Paola continued, "I thought you might want some company, Shadowwalker. There aren't many female warriors, so we might as well stick together." She sent another smile toward Ash, who returned a slight one. "And besides, I thought you might want this back." She produced the leather knapsack that Ash had worn during her attempted escape. Paola dug through it and pulled out the simple calfskin book. Ash's heart raced as she stared in horror, watching what the she-elf would do.

Paola laughed, a silvery tinkle that floated through the air.

"Don't worry, hombre, I won't tell anyone you have this Book, but you should be careful about who sees it." Paola winked and returned the Book to the bag. "I'll keep this with me until you get settled in a room." She stood up and began to leave with the tray. "And I heard about that fight with Alaistair. Nice job. If you ever need fighting lessons, find me and I'll help you kick his butt." The elf laughed once more and was gone.

The next morning, Ash was moved upstairs to an actual bedroom. One of the guards had picked her up with a grunt and quickly deposited her on the bed, sweating from the effort and leaving with shaking arms. Ash had frowned. She was only seventy-two kilograms and mostly muscle; Gill had been able to pick her up fine. The she-elf swept in after the man had left and smiled, her eyes shimmering with mirth.

"I guess Rifky should work on his arms that he boasts about." Paola laughed and then put on what Ash guessed to be a serious face for the short warrior. She closed the door and took out the Book, placing it underneath the other pillow on the bed. "I told the cleaners not to come in here until you are well enough to walk around the castle, so as to give you privacy. That will give you a day or two to hide this Book of yours." She winked her face back to its normal cheerfulness. "That poison really knocked you out, didn't it?"

Ash grimaced at the memory of the arrow sinking into her flesh. "Had I known it was poison, I would have pulled it out," she replied stoutly.

"Oh!" Paola faked a surprised face. "So the Mistress Arcop does speak!"

Ash made another face and sighed. Was she ever going to get used to that cursed title?

"I'd rather you call me Shadowwalker, please," she informed Paola with a pleading tone.

Paola nodded and clapped her shoulder, much like Carmel used to do, and left.

Ash smiled and, as the sun finally rose completely above the mountains, turned back to her room. Today was the first day she had most of her mobility back and she was determined to make the most of that day. The day before, she had hidden the Book in her desk and now didn't have to worry about it anymore.

Ash walked to the bathroom and started the shower, warming up the water as she stripped. The water was achingly warm and cleaned off the rest of the grime from the past week. She looked for soap for her long locks and found a sweet-smelling one. As she poured it on her hair, she glanced down to see her legs covered in a light mat of hair. Ash groaned and found a razor to shave off the annoying hair. After a long, therapeutic shower, she walked out and put on some new clothes. She had worn the same clothes for a week and was ready for a definite change. Throwing her old, ruined clothes into the fire, Ash put on black leggings and topped them with a fire-red sleeveless tunic that hit her mid-thigh. She added a white belt and put her hair into a high braid that snaked to her waist.

There was a knock at the door. Ash opened the door and stepped back quickly as Paola rushed in with the silver-haired man in tow. The man stopped in the middle of the room and scanned it nervously.

"Paola!" Ash began, used to the girl's energetic nature. "What are you doing here?"

The elf bounced over to her and took Ash's scared hands into her own petite ones.

"We are getting you out and about today!" She squealed like a young girl who was going to her first festival.

"This is a dumb idea, elfie," the silver-haired man said, his menacing face looking at Ash rather than Paola. "We don't know what she is capable of."

The elf turned to her friend and grabbed his arm.

"Kogu, it is going to be fine. It is a tour of the house." She licked her lips before continuing. "If you want, you can tell Alaistair that it was my idea and you just went along with it because it would be good to have a mage along in this dangerous expedition." She made a face and laughed as Kogu scoffed, smiling slightly. Then, taking Ash's arm, the she-elf led her out, talking a mile a minute about the infrastructure and different rooms of the house. Kogu trailed them, grumbling about the stupidity of the whole situation.

A few hours later, Ash and the two warriors were seated in a small flower garden, drinking coffee and eating some sandwiches that the cook, a man named Richard Tucket who had the portly figure of one who spends a lot of time near food, had scrounged up. The mage had relaxed and had struck up a conversation with the elf, who had yet to stop speaking. Ash studied the two of them and how they were completely comfortable with each other, not caring about rank or what was appropriate. Ash felt a twinge of sadness. She had never felt that level of comfort with anyone. Even with Gill there had always been rules about her interactions with him. She was roused from her thoughts when Kogu asked her a question. Those all-too-smart amber eyes fixed on her.

"I'm sorry," Ash's face reddened. "I missed what you said."

He sighed and rolled his eyes like she was a misbehaving child.

"I asked if you wanted to spar some," he said in a staccato rhythm.

She nodded and Paola erupted.

"Oh, wonderful!" she exclaimed. "Let's go now! I have wanted to ask you how good you were with a blade, but there was too much to talk about." Paola giggled. "Maybe Alaistair will be there too!"

Ash looked amusedly at the bouncing girl before her and wondered, not for the first time, how she was a warrior.

She then looked at the walls surrounding the castle, feeling penned-in. Ash steeled her heart. She would persevere, no matter these people might throw at her. With that, Ash stood and followed Paola and Kogu toward the entrance of the house, listening to their animated conversation. The mage actually looked like he was enjoying the elf's presence.

TWITTERPATED

The trio soon was at the training arena. Paola helped Ash into some fitted training clothes: black pants and a matching shirt which were a bit tight and short on Ash.

"Sorry," Paola excused. "I couldn't find any other clean clothes that would fit you better than mine would. Maybe next time?"

Ash shook her head, smiling gently.

"It's fine, Paola. I'll manage."

The elf looked quite relieved and quickly changed into another pair of her training clothes and turned to Ash. The two of them walked out of the female changing room to an annoyed Kogu.

"What do you guys do in there that takes so long?" he asked incredulously.

"Trust me, you don't want to know," a rich voice answered.

Ash turned and saw that it belonged to Alaistair, who was dressed in similar clothing along with—her heart stopped—Fross.

The two of them came closer and Paola hailed.

"Hey, Fross! Alaistair!" She waved, smiling like a little child. "We thought Ash should get some exercise after her week in bed."

Alaistair took in the three of them and said, "I have already practiced today. Rifky said something about needing to be able to pick up maidens." His brow crinkled in confusion about the mage's comment. "So I'll leave you two with the master."

Paola whined, making Ash chuckle, while Kogu nodded and Alaistair left.

"It looks like having you around will bring more than a little change," Paola whispered in Ash's ear, who smiled until she saw Fross.

She stepped up to him with a challenge in her gaze.

"Will you do me the honour, Sir Arcop," her voice took on a sarcastic tone at the last words, "to spar with me?"

Fross quirked an eyebrow in her direction, an infuriating move for Ash because she could not do it as smoothly as he could. "I thought we were going to drop all pretenses," he said, coolly walking over to a roped arena.

Ash followed him, hands clenched.

"But since you asked oh-so nicely," he paused, eyes flashing, "I suppose I will accept."

She began to square off, raising her light sword, but he wasn't finished.

"As long as you make a deal with me."

Ash's blade faltered slightly.

"What deal?" she ground out, looking with red-hot fury at his eyes.

"If I win," he began, unsheathing his own sword, "you have dinner with me tonight. And if you win, then you don't have to see my face for the rest of the week."

"The week ends today," Ash replied. "I'm not that unaware."

"But the deal stands," he replied. "You only have to say yes."

Ash thought about it. *He killed my family and I could get some answers from him.* She lunged for him but he parried the blow. The fight had started.

Fross smiled a cool smile. "I guess that is a yes."

They fought for the better part of an hour, with the fight in Ash's favour. He had knocked her in the cheek with the crossguard of his sword, making her drop her own sword. She retaliated by knocking him to his knees with a swipe of her leg. She wiped the blood from her mouth and cheek and picked up her sword. His eyes followed her with amusement, but he did not stand up. She pressed the blade to his neck.

"I win," she said exultingly. Ash looked around but the training room was deserted except for them.

He fixed her with the stare of an ice dragon and then moved with a speed and force that Ash was not expecting. He knocked the blade away from his throat and flipped her onto her back, crouching, with a small blade, by her neck.

"Think again, Shadowwalker," he said with a bite in his voice. "I'll see you at dinner." Fross gathered the equipment while Ash ran to her room, not wanting him to see her cry.

She opened her eyes and saw a flash of green hair. *Paola.* She looked up with her red-rimmed eyes at the gentle warrior. Paola hugged her with enthusiasm.

"It'll be all right, chica," she soothed Ash as she hiccuped from her sobs. She had been hearing them all afternoon and knew that it was about more than just losing to Fross. "Let's get you into something fit for tonight." She led Ash into the bathroom and filled up the tub as Ash stripped behind her.

As the shadowwalker bathed, she watched the she-elf pick out a graceful black dress, designed to hit her at the knees, and cringed.

"Paola," she said hesitantly. The little elf turned. "Could you pick out something other than black for tonight? I . . . I can't wear that colour tonight." She looked pleadingly at the warrior, who nodded.

For someone who was so silly, the elf was full of wisdom and understood the connection that Ash had made to the colour. She picked out a chocolate brown dress with a calf-length skirt, three-quarter sleeves, and a boat-neck collar. Paola looked at the younger girl and raised the dress in a silent question. She nodded and the elf hung it on a hook close to the tub and left.

"I'll be out here waiting for you, chica," she called in her cheery voice.

Ash got out of the tub and quickly got dressed, putting on the dress and matching gloves that covered the transparent white scars.

As she walked into the bedroom, she saw Paola bring out a pair of gladiator sandals, which she then put on. The elf looked at her new friend, her violet eyes pulsing as she thought.

"Do you want makeup or something else?" she asked Ash, who shook her head.

"I'd rather not wear that stuff. It makes me really itchy," Ash confessed.

Paola linked their arms and patted her hand.

"It's all right, chica. You don't need to hide anything." She gazed concernedly at Ash. She had seen the myriad of scars and knew that not all of those had been accidental. "You are safe here."

Ash turned her head and met her new friend's gaze with fear. "Am I?"

And with that unanswered question hanging in the air, Paola escorted her to the small dining room, just right for a small number of people.

They stopped at the entrance of the room and Ash sucked in a breath. *Just breathe, there is nothing to fear.* But Ash knew this had less to do with fear than nervousness. *I shouldn't be nervous. He is just a man.* Pushing the feeling away from her thoughts, she looked down at the little elf, who gave her another encouraging smile and pushed open the doors.

The room held a table that was large enough for six people but was only set for two, at opposite ends of the table. The chairs were cushioned with light gold fabric and wood trim. Ash's dress fit in with the colour scheme to the point that it was as if the room had been created for her. *Probably Paola's doing.* Ash hadn't known the girl for long, but she wouldn't be surprised if the warrior had had a hand in this. The room had large double doors, much like the ones in her room, that went out to the garden right underneath her own balcony. She walked over to the doors, curious as to what was in the garden. As she lifted her gloved hand to open the door, someone cleared their throat. Ash whirled around to see Fross, in a pair of black pants and a cream-coloured vest over a black shirt with a chocolate-coloured cravat, standing in a corner of the room. *Apparently, someone informed him of my clothing choice*, thought Ash as she marched closer to him.

"Don't expect me to curtsy or act like a lady just because you dressed up," she said, with what she hoped was a fiery tone. He gave her his infuriating smirk and gestured to the table laden with a light soup.

"Then let us get to eating," he said, in a slightly amused voice.

She stomped over to the table and plopped down in a seat. He took his seat opposite her at the table. She mentally sent a quick prayer to the Creator for the food and remembered what she had read in the Book: *Do to others as you would do to yourself and love your neighbour as yourself.* Ash cringed. She wasn't acting much like how she knew the Creator would want her to act, but she didn't want to love this man in any sort of way. *I should at least try, though.* Her temper relented, and she began to eat the thin broth. She looked at the man before her with new eyes. He was handsome but seemed to be cold and calculating. At that second, he caught her gaze, and she quickly returned it to the bowl of cooling soup. The silence was uncomfortable now and Ash racked her brain for some type of topic of conversation.

"The soup is very nice," she said, cringing at the lameness of the topic. "The cook did a wonderful job balancing the flavours."

There was a slight chuckle and she looked up to see Fross looking at her, with a slight smile gracing his even lips.

"Yes, Richard does a very good soup. It was ingrained in him by his family from a very young age." His eyes twinkled at his response. "Be careful not to eat too much, there still is more to come."

Ash was surprised at the politeness in his voice. *Well, maybe if I'm pleasant, then he'll return the favour. What a novel idea*, she thought sarcastically to herself as she went back to eating the soup.

As Fross had said, there were multiple courses. Ash ate, trying all the different foods as she and Fross made stilted conversation about absolutely nothing. Well, stilted for Ash. Fross seemed to glide through every response with the grace of a swimmer, which infuriated Ash as she tried to reign in her temper.

After the last dish had been taken away, Fross rose and Ash copied him, thinking the night was done and she could return to her quarters. She was mistaken. Instead of leaving, Fross crossed to her side of the table and reached out a hand. She looked at her own gloves, which were stained from the meal, and looked at him, hesitating. He gave her a look that was a mixture of impatience and curiosity and took her hand.

"Why are you doing this?" she asked him, looking at his eyes. "You killed my family, and now through kindness are you trying to make me forget?"

He looked at her with something akin to gentleness, but it passed quickly and he sighed, irritated.

"I did not kill your family, Shadowwalker. How many times must I tell you that?"

Until I believe you. The words were on her tongue but she swallowed them and said nothing.

He took her out to the garden and as she stepped out through the doors her heart calmed itself. For the first time that night, she relaxed. Ash slipped her hand from his warm grasp and went to look at her favourite bush, a white rose bush on the side of the garden. She reached for one of the roses, but then stopped and turned toward Fross.

"May I take one?" she asked, trying to keep her voice from trembling.

"Of course," he replied, gesturing to the garden. "This entire garden is yours if you wish."

Ash snorted. "You don't have to ply me with gifts, Slayer. I simply wanted to pick a rose for my room."

He shrugged, a movement both uncaring and condescending, and put his hands in his pockets. Ash quickly snatched a white rose and stepped back, noticing too late that a thorn had scratched through her glove and caused her to bleed.

"What's that?" the melodic voice inquired with a hint of concern as Fross walked over to her.

"Oh, so now you are concerned?" she asked sarcastically. "You made me bleed during sparring. Didn't seem to care then."

Fross, ignoring her barb, took her hand and ripped off the glove. Ash pulled her hand from his grip and hid it with her other hand.

"I think I'm going to go to bed now," Ash said, stepping back quickly. "Good night."

Ash ran to her room and sat down on her bed, shaking. *I can't get so close; he's too dangerous, even if he didn't kill my family.* She looked down at her hands and took off the other glove. The white scars covered her hands, looking like flames and ending just past her wrists. She closed her eyes, letting a single tear pass, and fell back on her bed. *Help me, Creator*, was her last thought as she fell asleep.

******

Fross looked at the path Ash had taken. The glove was strangled in his fist. She was scared of him for some reason and he was surprised that she had even come to dinner. But as she had run away, he'd seen the scars stamped on her hand. He now understood why her hands were always hidden in gloves, tucked away from the world. They were scarred after what looked to be hours beneath flames. His ice-cold rage flooded his body. *What beast would hurt her like that?* Fross spotted the rose that, in her flight, had fallen to the ground and picked it up. His rage left him as he stared at the flower and planned out what he would do.

It had been ages since he'd been down in the kitchen, but the scents reminded him of memories that he thought had been long lost. He cleared his throat to get the attention of the cook, who turned and jumped at the sight of his master.

"Lord Fross!" the tubby man said, bowing in an awkward bow. "I didn't hear you come in."

Fross grimaced. *Was this what his servants thought of him? That they must tremble at his approach?* The thought of it sickened him slightly.

"Yes, I came down to thank you for the spread. It was quite lovely and delicious. The shadowwalker genuinely enjoyed the soup, so give her some for breakfast, along with this." Fross produced the flower. "Put it in something nice for the lady." He sighed, went outside, and looked at the moon, feeling better than normal.

Cafuné

The sun beamed through the window and onto Ash's face, waking her up. She got up and saw her reflection, with mussed hair and rumpled clothes from the night before. She smiled, thinking about the silliness of her look, and turned to get dressed for the day. She picked out a light-emerald skirt and a cream long-sleeved shirt, with little green gloves for her hands. At the sound of a knock, she walked across the floor, thinking it was probably Paola. Ash opened the door and saw only a small cart, with a tray covered by a silver lid. She pulled it inside and placed the tray on a table. She spotted a white rose in a small blue vase. A small smile tugged at her lips. *Maybe I can tame the beast in that man.* She uncovered the dish and laughed, seeing the soup from the night before. *Yes*, she thought to herself, *today looks to be a good day.*

Ash had finished the soup and had begun making a new copy of the Book, her pen strokes creating clear and concise letters, when she looked at the clock. She had been up for three hours and had heard no one bustling in the castle, nor had Paola burst through her door. The hairs on the back of Ash's neck rose. Something wasn't right.

Ash snuck through the castle with silent grace and saw nobody. She went through the castle, level by level, and as she checked out the level above the dungeon, she heard a small scrape. The shadowwalker froze in her tracks. Had that been a knife? She heard it again and turned to the noise. It was coming from down the hall, where the boiler room was. She padded down the hallway and saw the faintest light under the crack in the door as if someone had tried to block it from coming through. Ash walked past that door and to the next one. She slipped through into a dark room. In a corner, she saw a small window that faced the room she had just passed. Ash crept to the window and, peeking through it, saw a meeting in session. There were six of the guards, the warrior trio, and Fross, all sitting around a circular table. One of the guards—Vala, Ash thought her name was; a middle-aged human with already-white hair and brown eyes set deep in her face—was giving a report about the perimeter wall being secure and about the last few trespassers who had tried to scale it.

Ash listened to this for several minutes until the meeting took a turn. Once Vala had finished, Fross broached the one topic Ash was not prepared for: the Cartier investigation. At the sound of her maiden name, she gasped ever-so slightly. Not loudly, but loud enough that Paola heard it. The elf stood up abruptly and said, "We are not alone."

There was the screeching sound from the chairs as the entire group rose and turned in the direction that Paola had pointed.

Ash turned to flee but was stopped by Alaistair, who had somehow gotten behind her.

Ash was dragged into the room and Fross nodded a greeting to her as he brought another chair to put between him and Paola. Ash took her place at his left hand and the meeting continued as if it hadn't been interrupted. They continued to talk about the different aspects of the attack such as the manner in which it had been done, the body count, and the methods of fighting the assassins had employed.

Ash realized that she had blamed the wrong man and she reminded herself to talk to him about it afterwards.

After whispering something to Alaistair, Paola took Ash's hand, under the table, and gave it a gentle squeeze, as if to say she was not alone. Ash appreciated the gesture. She was feeling very small while surrounded by the warriors and trained guards. She turned her attention back to the group when the mage, Kogu, said in an irritated voice, "If only we could see their plans and where they are hiding now. The Black Eagles Gang, or B.E.G. as they liked to be called, have to be behind this. They left their mark." He threw a picture of what looked to be a circle divided into thirds, with the letters *B.E.G.* on it. Kogu put his hands on the table, bracing himself as he looked into his compatriots' eyes. "I could find a powerful mage that could foresee their next attack." He looked toward Fross. "With your permission, of course."

Ash looked at Fross, who was about to give permission to his spellcaster, when Ash said, "No."

All eyes suddenly shifted to her. Some curious, others surprised, and a few downright opposed to her presence. Ash felt her cheeks redden. *It was now or never.*

"Don't go to a foreseer," she said, as her mind stumbled to create sentences that held reason. "To see the future isn't an ability given to us. Only the foolish try, and they fail. I understand your desire to find these animals." She turned to look at Kogu, and then to her betrothed. "But I assure you, this plan will fail if you go through with it, and you might be sending people to their death."

"Who is she, that she thinks we will listen to her?" asked the guard Noah, the brother of Haon. They were identical, with the same green hair and pink eyes that marked them as elf twins, which were very rare. Their only difference was that Noah had a long scar running across his face, from forehead to jawline. This scar made him look very dangerous when he scowled, as he did then at Ash, who shrank back a bit.

"She can be trusted," said Fross in a leader's voice, gesturing for Noah to sit down and calm himself. He turned to study Ash. "If you don't wish us to go to a foreseer, then what do you expect us to do?" he queried in a softer voice.

Ash inhaled shakily.

"Go back to the castle. It is still standing, isn't it?" She looked for confirmation from Paola, who nodded. "Check for more evidence as to where they went. If you were able to find where they came in, you could find out where they went. Just follow the tracks."

Alaistair sighed slightly.

"We have, Shadowwalker, but there were barely any tracks to find." He paused, pain flitting through his face, before continuing in his rich voice. "Many people tried to make it out of the castle during the attack. Most weren't so lucky. There aren't any tracks to be found except for those of the sellswords who went after you."

Ash paled at the memory of killing them to save her own life and nodded.

"I might know someone who could help your predicament," she stated.

The meeting continued on after that, with plans for finding her tracker, Gill, and other matters that had been on the list of topics, without any more interruptions from Ash. She simply sat there and watched how everybody interacted with each other. They didn't use titles down here, which made it seem as if it was a group of people who were very comfortable with each other. It was refreshing for Ash, who had always hated the titles that had been forced on her as a chieftain's daughter.

Soon, the meeting was over and people began to leave. Paola stood up and waited for Ash to rise. Ash did so but whispered to the elf that she was going to stay back and discuss something with Fross. Paola's pink eyebrows rose in surprise but she nodded, smiling impishly, and left with the promise of an anti-Alaistair training that afternoon if Ash was interested. The shadowwalker waved her friend goodbye and turned to Fross, who was talking about some small strategy with Alaistair. The second-in-command bowed slightly—the first time that Ash had seen any show of respect that resembled her own family's culture—and left, following Paola. Then Fross turned his gaze toward her, and her heart began to beat ever-so-slightly faster.

There was something different about Fross but Ash hadn't been able to put her finger on it. Now that he'd turned around, Ash saw it.

"What happened to your ha- ?"

"I lost a bet," he replied before she could finish her question.

Surprised that he would even gamble, she asked: "Why?"

He sighed and turned away.

"I don't want to talk about it." His voice was irritable and it made Ash smile slightly. *He's embarrassed about his hair.* She shifted gears and said, "I simply wanted to say I'm sorry."

This made him turn around and she saw the damage. His long hair had been cut into a style in which his hair rested at chin length. Ash decided that she liked it better at that length than halfway down his back, and met his inquisitive gaze.

"I blatantly assumed you were the one responsible for my parents' death and didn't give you the chance to explain yourself." She continued, grasping his hand. "I also was very unkind to you when we first met. Perhaps we could start over fresh or at least put it behind us."

He smiled a real smile that made her stomach flutter.

"Yes, Shadowwalker, I would like that very much."

They walked out of the basement together, and only then did Ash realize that she was still holding his hand. Letting go, she stepped slightly to the side, allowing there to be more space in between their bodies. He looked at her with an expression that conveyed slight hurt and confusion. She looked down and said nothing as they continued to walk.

"Come with me," he demanded, as they reached a flight of stairs that would lead to her room. Fross grabbed Ash's arm and began to take her past the stairs. "I have something to show you."

And with that, Ash felt herself being dragged to another door that led out into a field. She noticed what Fross was wearing: sturdy brown pants and a green shirt with a leather vest on top of it. He rolled up his sleeves, displaying his muscular, caramel forearms. He attached leather gauntlets to his arms and let out a piercing whistle. There was a screech, and two falcons, one a snowy white and another ash black, descended onto his protected arms. They made a weird chirping sound and looked at Fross expectantly.

He chuckled.

"Easy there, guys. There is someone I want you to meet."

The two falcons turned to eye Ash who let out a gasp.

"They are beautiful," she whispered in awe. She reached out to pet the white one, who let her touch its plumage.

"That one is Myr," he said, gesturing to the white one. Turning his attention to the black one: "This one's name is Fye. He's Myr's mate and my personal falcon." The falcons stayed for a little while and then flew off toward the mountains.

Ash looked at Fross with a new understanding.

"Thank you for showing me them, they seem to be very precious to you," she said, looking at the ground, all of a sudden bashful.

"Yes, they are one of the few things that are precious to me," he said. Ash looked up to see him gazing at her and turned to the door.

"I have a lesson with Paola I should be getting to," was all she answered him, hurrying off to the training centre.

Basorexia

The afternoon went by quickly for Ash. Paola showed her new techniques and skills for hand-to-hand combat. For her small size, Paola was surprisingly strong and fierce during combat. After her hundredth time hitting the mat, Ash decided to call it a day and went to her room to wash off the sweat and add cream that had been given to her by Blanche, a skillful alchemist, to her bruises. The bruise cream, also known as icofoxin temonadryl, smelled minty and felt cool when Ash applied it after her short shower.

She had put on some comfortable clothes—baggy pants and a long shirt, without gloves—when there was a knock at the door. Ash opened it and Paola swept in, decked out in a mint-green dress that went with her hair and with accessories in a corresponding shade of pink. She also wore black eyeliner that swept out at the corner of her eyes, making them seem more catlike. She stopped, surprised that Ash was in those clothes.

"Where are your clothes, chica?" she asked, her accent rolling its *r*s again. At the confused look on Ash's face, she prodded her memory. "Don't you remember me telling you that there is a dinner for high command? That includes you now."

Ash ran to her bathroom and brought out a blue dress the colour of a darkening twilight.

"Will this work?" she asked, already unbuttoning her shirt.

The elf rolled her eyes.

"Yes, that will work just fine. Now go in there and put it on."

Ash didn't need any more encouragement. Within a minute, she had slipped into the ballroom-style dress and the appropriate gloves for such a dress. Scooting into some blue shoes, Ash quickly followed Paola out the door, praying they wouldn't be late.

******

By the time Ash and Paola arrived at the feast in the garden, all the men had arrived. Alaistair and Kogu wore suits with ties the same colour as their hair. Fross wore a suit similar to that of his friends, with a cravat that balanced the two shades of brown in his eyes and a white rose in his lapel. Ash smiled at seeing him dressed with a discreet nod to her own preferences and walked over to him.

"You look well-put-together," she announced, cringing as the words that had sounded nice in her head came out in an awkward fashion.

He smiled with age-old amusement and replied, "As do you, my lady."

His lady. Ash decided she could let that one slide. It did sound nice coming from his mouth.

"Are we going to eat yet? The girls took forever to get here and now she's waylaying the feast even more!" groused Kogu, crossing his arms. He would have said more but was elbowed by both Alaistair and Paola, and wisely stopped speaking.

But the moment was already shattered. They sat down to eat: Fross at the head of the table, Alaistair on his left, and Ash on his right, with Paola beside her and the grumbling mage by Alaistair, across from the pretty elf.

The meal started like the dinner the night before had, with soup. But unlike the night before, there were no awkward silences or conversation topics. Instead, boisterous voices filled the air, along with laughter. Stories were exchanged and, for the first time in a long while, Ash felt at home. She laughed with Paola, traded jabs with Alaistair, and cheered up Kogu.

Once, when they were dining on a succulent roasted lamb with a mint-and-lemon salad that Kogu detested, Ash brushed Fross's arm. She sucked in a breath and stole a glance at him, wondering if she was the only one who felt a slight tingle at the contact. Fross was caught up in witty banter with Kogu; his face betrayed nothing. Ash settled down and began to eat her lamb with gusto again, only to almost choke on a small piece when Fross's hand lightly skimmed the outside of her thigh, on top of the blue material. Going almost completely red, Ash made sure to keep her hands away from Fross for the rest of the dinner.

Soon, out came a lovely treat that Paola claimed they only got once a year.

"It's iced cream that Richard makes," she chirped happily, digging her spoon into the light-brown dessert. "He flavours it with coffee and it is so frothy that even a person as picky as Kogu falls in love with it."

Kogu's head snapped up from staring at the treat before him.

"I'm not picky!" he grumbled, cheeks reddening slightly. "I just have better self-control of what I chose to put in my mouth. Not all of us put it away like pigs." He looked pointedly at his two companions.

"Picky," whispered Paola, giggling in Ash's ear.

"I heard that!" shouted Kogu, and the two of them were at it again.

Ash watched, chuckling slightly, and turned her gaze to the melting treat in front of her. Someone patted her left arm and she looked up to see Fross looking at her.

"Eat it slowly and save yourself a headache later," he instructed, grinning. "It's more fun to watch someone else experience the brain freeze than to experience it yourself." He nodded to Alaistair, who had finished his iced cream and now held his head in his hands, groaning softly while Paola stood behind him, patting his shoulders soothingly.

Fross and Ash chuckled, and she bit into her dessert. It was cool and creamy, like a glass of fresh cream, and the soft flavour of coffee made Ash want to gobble it all. But she listened to Fross's instruction and ate it slowly, not wanting to feel the wrath of whatever Alaistair was feeling.

The dishes were cleared away and Paola began pulling Ash by the arm. She looked at her bouncing friend, once again confused.

"The night has just begun, chica! It's the summer solstice and we have plans!"

"What type of plans?" asked Ash nervously.

"Big ones!" replied the elf, who pulled Ash out of her chair and back to the house.

******

A few minutes later, Ash and Paola were outfitted in black, loose clothing, perfect for moving in.

"Why do you guys wear so much black?" Ash asked, disgusted by the colour.

"It makes us blend into our surroundings easier, and it hides sweat during training sessions," said the she-elf, practically. "It isn't because of any weird reason or cultural habit. Just practical."

The ladies went toward a large field covered with different obstacles and trees.

"Hah!" the elf exclaimed. "We are the first ones here this time."

Ash looked around. Indeed they were.

"What are we going to be doing?" she asked Paola, whose green hair glowed slightly in the darkening sky.

"Oh, we are going to be playing hide-and-seek," she responded with a shrug of her shoulders. "It is a really fun game . . . at least the way we play is."

Ash was about to ask her more when Fross came into view. He saw her and smiled like a little boy getting his first sword.

"Do you need me to tell you the rules, or did Paola already spoil it for me?" he teased, eyes sparkling with excitement.

"I didn't tell her anything!" yelled the elf as she bounded over to talk with Kogu and Alaistair.

Ash chuckled and caught the strange look Fross gave her.

"So, Paola and Alaistair?" she asked.

Fross smiled and looked at his friends chatting with each other.

"Yep, that has been going on for ages. They never get tired of each other."

Ash nodded, sensing the wistfulness in his voice. *Maybe he is human after all.*

Fross turned and began his instructions for the game.

"The rules are simple," he began. "There are two teams. Everyone has a meson pistol filled with either blue or red bioluminescent ink. Each team is then divided into two groups: hiders and seekers. The hiders hide while the seekers seek. Once you are shot, you are allowed to hunt all members of the opposing team. The goal is to shoot as many of the reds or blues as possible before time runs out. Do you understand?"

Ash nodded. "Shoot the other side and don't get shot."

Fross smiled. *What a girl*, he thought. He then went to address the crowd of his guards and servants, all dressed in the same black garb.

"Do not shoot for the head or up close. Shoot to mark and not to hurt. This is a game of strength, skill, and virtue. Play with all of those or don't play at all," he barked out to them. They nodded in response and he smiled.

Paola and Kogu passed out to the crowd ties of red or blue. Alaistair was head of the red team and Fross of the blue. Ash smiled when she was given a red sash. As much as she enjoyed Fross's company, she still had a lesson to teach him for beating her in combat. Though Alaistair had done the same thing to her, Ash believed that he had suffered enough from the iced cream. It was time for sweet, silly revenge.

The teams were sent to either side of the field and the timer was set by the cook, who no longer played in the games due to the unusual number of times he would get shot.

"I'm a cook, not a warrior. I'll leave the games to you," he'd always huff, leaving the field covered in as much red as blue. He now sat on the sidelines and kept watch of the time.

While the other women on her team were sent to hide, Ash was selected as a seeker, along with Haon Prideblazer, who owned pink eyes and a full head of shocking green hair. The women grumbled about being left out of the fun, but when Alaistair pointed out that their hair was more likely to glow than the hair of their male counterparts, they left in silence, not wanting to lose the game.

Ash waited with bated breath as the minutes ticked by. *One, two, three, four, five.* Then a shout went out from Richard, who was sitting safely on the sidelines, that sounded very much like, "Go get them!"

The game had started and Ash knew who her target was.

******

It was five minutes into the game and Ash had finally found him. He was good, she'd give him that much, but he was no match for her silent stalking.

He had found Paola and was about to fire when someone got him between the shoulder blades. He spun to see who had shot, but no one was around. Fross grunted, went back, and shot Paola in the leg. As he ran away as he looked for one woman in particular. *Ash.* Her name was on his lips but he dare not say it. It was too special and precious for him to say. He had stopped running, in order to listen, and then he heard it: a slight hum in the air. He crouched too late and was hit by another splotch of red. He whirled around and shot toward the direction from which the projectile had come. Fross heard his shot hit its target and went after the moving blue splotch like a dragon after a human.

He got me, thought Ash as she ran through the trees and jumped over an old mattress. She hid behind a barrel that bore the brand from which Arcop Manor residents got most of their clothing, Mirage Couture, and cocked her gun. She could make four more shots before heading back to base to reload. She was going to make them count. The sound of footsteps reached her ears and she popped her head above the barrel. She saw a silhouette with red paint on him. She aimed and shot, hitting her target just as someone hit her in the back. She looked up to see an athletic form with green hair and a blue sash running away. *You're next, Noah*, she promised, but this was one promise she wasn't going to make good on.

Fross felt the third shot hit his chest. He looked and saw a brown braid on a barrel. *Got you!* he thought, and raced toward the barrel. He tackled Ash just as she had risen to run after someone else. She yelped in surprise and then laughed as her adrenaline raced through her. *What a beautiful laugh she has.*

Ash looked at Fross's face, shining from sweat and with a sweet grin plastered on his face. She pushed his sweaty bangs from his forehead and leaned back onto the grass.

"I think I win this time," she said, grinning.

He flashed her a heart-warming grin and replied, "Who has who on the ground?"

They chuckled and Ash leaned up to bump his nose with hers like she had done with Gill so many years ago. As she got closer, she noticed he'd stopped breathing. His eyes had gone wide as he stared at her. At that moment, before she bumped his nose, he looked more like a young man than a master of a castle. She quickly bumped his nose and fell back onto the soft grass. He stared at her as if in shock for a moment or two and then rolled off of her. They lay there in silence for a while, just listening to each other breathe.

"You are surprisingly good at this game," Fross finally said, propping himself up on one arm to look at the beauty beside him.

She looked at him and rolled her eyes in a way that only Ash could do.

"You aren't that bad yourself," she admitted.

He chuckled.

"Yes, but I've been playing it longer than you have."

"Yeah, but you aren't that much my senior, maybe a year or two. How old are you?" she asked, pinning him with her blue eyes.

She watched him pause for a second, close his eyes and say, "Twenty."

"See? That's only a year older than me," she pointed out. "I'm nineteen."

He looked at Ash and was about to say something when the buzzer sounded. Fross got up and held out a hand for Ash, who ignored it and got up by herself. He was not that surprised: Ash would only do something if she wanted to do it. He liked that about her.

They walked back to the cook side-by-side. They were not holding each other's hands but both wanted to do so.

By the time they had made it back, the rest of the teams had already assembled. When they saw the two of them, they clapped and cheered.

"Welcome back, slowpokes!" yelled the cook. A few people laughed, but most looked toward Fross to see his reaction. When he smiled and waved, the teams burst out laughing and slapped each other's backs before slipping away to bed.

Paola informed Ash that she was going to sleep and Ash began to follow her. Fross grabbed her arm and pulled her close to him.

"Please stay," he begged, his eyes boring into Ash's. "At least for a little while."

Ash looked back at the she-elf, who was with Alaistair and halfway across the field to the house, and looked back to the nervous, young man in front of her.

"All right," she whispered, leaning in closer. "Just for a little while."

Osculate

Ash's heart pounded in her ears as Fross led her up two flights of stairs to a closed, ornate door. His hand shook as he turned the knob to let them in.

"This is my room," he said, walking in backwards.

Ash gasped as she entered. It took up an entire corner of the third floor!

"It's amazing!" she breathed, walking over to one of the floor-to-ceiling windows.

His footsteps sounded behind her as he closed the distance.

"Yes," his voice whispered in her ear. "It is."

Ash turned to look at him as he licked his lips, wanting to say more.

"I moved up here and made the room bigger once I knew I was getting married," he said anxiously, as if it wouldn't meet her standards.

She put her arms around his neck, feeling reckless, and bumped his nose again.

"It is perfect," she murmured, her gaze slowly dropping until she was looking at his lips. She wondered what it would be like to give in and kiss her betrothed just once.

Ash didn't have time to think. Her body betrayed her and curled around his as her lips slowly rose to his. She gave him a light kiss that stilled his breathing and broke away. *This is wrong!* she thought, and slowly backed away. His eyes fluttered open and his face took on a wild look.

"I'm sorry, Slayer." She stumbled on the words, pulling her body back under her control. "I shouldn't have done that."

Ash turned and ran, ignoring her betrothed's calls for her to stop.

She collapsed in her room, locked the door, and cried.

Why had she been so stupid?! He doesn't follow the Creator, and once he knew that she did, would he even care? Or was that all lust? It had felt like it on her part, and she had resolved to not be with a man if it was only lust.

Ash threw on her pyjamas and curled up in her bed, falling asleep as tears rolled down her face.

******

The morning was dark and grey, much like Ash's mood. She had had another weird dream about the man with the hooded, green eyes and it was beginning to irritate her. When she awoke, there was something not right. She had felt it when she woke up at the crack of dawn. The dread in the pit of her stomach hadn't lessened but had grown with every hour.

Ash finally decided she had had enough of the feeling and went to investigate. She followed, letting the feeling in her stomach guide her, much like in the dream. She crept up the stairs to the third floor and walked to Fross's room. The door opened to blood.

Ash gasped and ran in looking for the man. She found him by the toilet, lying on the floor, shuddering.

"Oh, Fross!" she whispered, and looked around the giant room. There was vomit everywhere. Fross shuddered again, the motion shaking his entire body. "Stay here, I'll get some help," whispered Ash as concern and dread bloomed within her. She took off running toward the one door where she knew someone could help.

There was a loud bang on his door and Alaistair awoke with a jolt. *What time was it?* He looked at the clock, it was barely nine in the morning. Groaning, he rolled out of bed and walked toward the door, shrugging on a privacy robe as he did. He opened his door and, to his surprise, saw Ash outside it.

"Please help me!" she begged, looking dishevelled to say the least. "Fross is sick and I don't know what to do."

Her eyes were full of unshed tears, but Ash wouldn't let herself cry. It would be tantamount to losing hope and she wouldn't. She followed the golden-haired giant as he ran to the healer's room. He banged on the door and was quickly rewarded with the healer in his nightcap at the door.

"Fross needs you," the giant growled. The healer nodded, fear lighting his eyes.

Ash watched Fross from the entrance of his room. Kogu and Alaistair had put him on his bed, wiping him down the best they could. The healer stumbled in, wearing rumpled clothing, along with his assistant. Both looked like raccoons had given them their masks. Ash worried the hem of her shirt while watching people swarm around her betrothed's still body. *Did I cause this?* she wondered, and was driven into her thoughts by worry.

The minutes crawled, but finally Fross came to. Weak but alive. Ash heard him instruct his people to leave him alone, and she had turned to go herself when Kogu grabbed her arm. His amber eyes softened and he said, "He wants you to stay." Kogu walked out the door as he said those last words. "Thank you for saving him."

Ash was surprised by the words but ran over to the bed. Fross's skin looked deathly pale and his eyes were wild with fear. He saw Ash standing there and the edge of the wildness was swept away.

"You came," he rasped, seeming to take all of his energy to say so little. She smiled and nodded, holding his hand.

"Yes, I'm here." Her face crumpled slightly. "Don't scare us like that again!"

Ash rose to leave but Fross's grip on her hand continued. She looked down at him.

"Please stay," he begged. "Don't leave me alone."

Ash's heart went out to him and so she sat on the side of his bed.

"Do you want me to tell you stories about my past?" she asked, gently brushing the hair from his eyes.

He nodded, his gaze not leaving her face.

******

Ash sighed. Fross was asleep. She had told him all the nice stories of her past and then delved into talking about the Creator when he had asked. The entire time his mismatched brown and green eyes had watched her as if she was the only thing between his life and death. She looked at the man now; he looked peaceful when he slept and the usual hardness in his face was gone, leaving the young man she had seen the night before.

Maybe I could love him. The thought just popped into her mind. Ash shook her head, that wouldn't happen. They were too different, eternal light and eternal darkness, fire and ice. Unless he was able to change on a deep level, there was no chance that they could work.

Ash slipped his head off its position on her lap, resting it back on his pillow. She fought the urge to kiss his forehead and left the room.

Not surprisingly, Paola found her and immediately brought her in for a tight hug.

"I'm sorry, chica," she whispered.

"It's okay, he will live," replied Ash, patting the elf's head.

The two broke apart and Ash went to freshen up again while Paola hunted down some food for them.

Ash had gotten out of the shower when she got that feeling. As she stood there wearing nothing but a towel, she felt it. That weird burning coursing through her veins. Except that this time it was stronger.

The golden light flashed around her and she heard only one thing before she fell into darkness: "I am with you, do not be afraid."

* * * * * *

Ash felt herself being shaken.

"Ash!" a voice yelled at her. "Wake up, please!"

She fluttered her eyes open to see violet eyes staring at her.

"What happened?" asked Paola as she helped the shadowwalker to her feet.

Ash hesitated, not knowing how much she should say.

"I just saw some stuff and got a bit dizzy." She shrugged to hide her discomfort.

The purple eyes studied her.

"Did you and Fross . . . ?" Paola trailed off, clearly embarrassed.

Ash, unsure of what her friend was asking, asked: "Did Fross and I what?"

Paola cleared her throat."You know, consummate?"

Ash's face reddened at the thought of that.

"No, we haven't. He's been a gentleman and we aren't married," she squeaked.

Paola looked relieved but also slightly sad.

"Do you know what the problem was?" Ash asked, remembering the blood on the floor.

"It happens every year," Paola said, her face going pale. "But it has never been that bad before."

"Any idea what caused it?"

"No, Fross won't tell us, which I'm sure doesn't surprise you." Paola let out a weak chuckle. "Before you came, he was terribly stubborn and prideful. But you have changed him so much in the past few weeks, it is amazing."

"I'm not the one who is doing it," Ash replied.

Paola looked at her quizzically and Ash continued. "Remember that Book I brought with me here? The One who authored that Book is the one who is doing this amazing thing."

Paola looked at her, confusion running amok across her face, and Ash began to tell her what the old man had told her so many years before.

Before Ash could ask her if she understood, there was a knock at the door.

"There is someone at the gate for the lady," the guard announced when Paola answered the door.

The elf looked at her with the same surprise that Ash herself was feeling.

Who could it be?

CINGULOMANIA

Ash walked toward the front gate, with the guard and Paola trailing her. Ash glanced in front of her and saw a flash of light blond curl. Her heart leapt. *It couldn't be, not so fast!*

Ash ran forward and threw her arms around the figure, a small squeal escaping her as he picked her up.

"Gill!" she screamed, inhaling the familiar scent of her old friend. *Dew and cinnamon, as always.*

"Hey, Ashy!" replied Gill, calling her by her nickname while swinging her around.

She laughed and her stress quickly dissipated. He set her down and ruffled her unbound hair.

"Got a hairdo I see," Gill pointed out, tugging a strand of Ash's wild hair, his amber eyes smiling. "But your guard dog doesn't seem to enjoy my presence."

Ash turned to where Gill was looking and saw Alaistair, with a deep furrow in his brow, marching over to them.

"Gillith Preslar," Alaistair greeted the tracker with a curt nod. "I'm glad you could arrive so quickly. Vincent," he gestured to the ginger guard with dreadlocks pulled back into a neat ponytail, who had escorted Ash, "will take you to your quarters." Turning to Ash, Alaistair said, "His Lordship wishes for your company."

Hearing that, Ash's heart sank slightly. She looked at Gill and saw a storm cloud in his hooded eyes. Turning back to face the giant, she responded, "Yes, I'll be there in a bit. I wish to spend some time with my friend first. Please send my regards to Fross." She paused for a second and asked, "How is he doing?"

Alaistair shrugged. "He's up and moving around, already restless about being cooped up and swearing he is back to full health. He heals quickly for a human."

Ash nodded, tucking that little bit of knowledge away.

"I'll be there later," she yelled back to Alaistair as she took Gill's arm, quickly walking to the house.

Once they were out of hearing distance of the elf, Ash asked, "How did they find you so fast?"

Gill shrugged, something that looked casual to the normal viewer, but Ash knew better. He was troubled.

"I just wanted to make sure you were okay."

Ash bumped his shoulder.

"Come on, Gill. I've known you since I was four and you were seven. What's really going on?"

Gill stopped and looked at Ash, who was almost his height, with a protective fierceness.

"I should have been there for your wedding, Ashy. I heard what happened. You shouldn't have witnessed that."

"Gill, I'm a warrior just like you," she reminded him and continued walking.

"I know, Ashy, but when it is your own parents . . ." He trailed off, a slight shimmer in his amber eyes.

Gill had watched his human father and mage mother be tortured and slaughtered for procreating. A crime that was punishable by death. He was forced to watch as a reminder of what would happen to him if he "contaminated" the bloodlines. Soon after, Gill showed up in Dasica at the Cartier Castle and had trained to be a warrior ever since.

Ash gulped, remembering his past life, and nodded, stopping in front of his room.

"If it makes you feel better, I didn't watch them die."

Gill's head whipped up from looking at the ground to study her, surprise flickering in his eyes.

"Paola, the she-elf, dragged me upstairs to my room and locked me inside," Ash said, looking at her friend with open concern. "Are you okay, Gill?"

He had paled from his normal coffee complexion to a light-coffee colour, his amber irises eclipsing the whites of his eyes. *Something is extremely wrong*, thought Ash. She had never seen him so frightened.

Gill grabbed her arm and pulled her into his room. He closed the door, locked it, and stood there for a long moment, not turning around. When he did turn around, Gill's eyes had gone back to normal somewhat, though the irises were still larger than normal.

"Have you gone back to the castle, Ash?" he asked, almost whispering.

Ash shook her head in response.

"You need to go back there, Ash," her friend continued, looking pained. "How did you even get out?"

Ash recounted her escape from the castle, with Gill looking even more concerned as she continued.

"Do you want to be here, Ash?" he asked her, looking deep into her eyes.

Ash hesitated. A week ago, she would have said yes, without a doubt, but now she wasn't so sure.

"I see," said Gill as he unlocked the door. "You should probably go before someone finds you in my room."

Ash looked at him, tears forming in her eyes.

"Gill," she began but he shook his head.

"Don't make excuses for what I saw. You care for him, someone who would kill you without hesitation if he knew what you are. Honestly, Ash, I thought you were better than that."

The words stung Ash but she refused to let it crush her.

"I don't think he would, not anymore," Ash said as she stepped out of the room. "And maybe you don't know me as well as you thought."

She walked back to her room, feeling her heart beginning to collapse again. But she didn't have time for that. She walked into her room and, seeing her bed, felt increasingly tired.

"Just a small rest," she told herself, and quickly fell asleep into a strange dream.

The ground was an undulating mass of fire that didn't burn her as she walked on it. A man showed up in front of her, smiling with perfect white teeth.

"Well, you are early," he said in his strange purring voice, his luminescent green eyes glowing.

"Tell me about Fross Arcop and the attack on Cartier Castle," demanded Ash.

He looked mildly bemused.

"Very well. Sit down." He gestured to some chairs behind them.

Ash plopped down, waiting.

"Fross Arcop is a manipulator and a great warrior, only bested by one," he began.

"Who?" Ash asked.

"The Creator, of course," he said, smiling. "Do you want me to continue?"

"Yes," Ash said, with more fire than the land around them.

His eyes glinted with malice as he began to speak once more.

* * * * * *

Ash awoke with rage in her. She looked at the clock to see it was past ten at night. The sun had just gone down and most of the residents would be asleep. *Perfect for what I must do*, she thought, grabbing from her drawer a gun that she had taken from the armoury.

Ash crept up the stairs to Fross's room. She had her hand on the doorknob when she heard voices inside.

"And when you are done with her," Gill's voice rumbled as much as a man with a higher voice could, "what will happen to her?"

There was a pause as Ash held her breath, waiting for an answer.

"Do you want her?" asked her betrothed, Fross. Ash felt all the air leave her lungs. They were deciding her future. "I can keep her if that is what you want, but you can have her."

You can have her. The words coursed through her as her rage exploded.

Ash threw open the door and stepped in to see a surprised Gill and a bored-looking Fross.

"Was it just an act, then?" yelled Ash as she began to raise the gun. "Get out of the way, Gill!"

Gill backed away from trying to calm down Ash.

Ash looked at Fross's mismatched eyes: "Survive this."

She pulled the trigger on the gun twice. Each time it jarred her until she dropped it after the second shot.

There was a yell of anger and anguish and Ash was thrown to the ground. She turned to see Alaistair looking down at her, eyes glowing molten gold with anger.

Ash gulped. Even though Paola had taught her some new fighting techniques, Alaistair had centuries of practice. He was faster, better, and stronger than her. But she was going to fight. The rage regrouped and focused on the giant and she jumped up to fight but never made it to her feet. A right hook from Alaistair sent her unconscious and she crumpled at his feet.

Alaistair looked at the girl in front of him, satisfied that she was out. He looked to see the blond boy trying to clean up his master. He pushed the boy out of the way, picked up Fross's still form, and ran to the healer's quarters.

"Come on, Fross. We need you now more than ever," said Alaistair as his feet pounded the planks.

******

"Don't tell me you are keeping her," said a deep voice a few hours later.

“Come on, Alaistair! She is harmless, don’t think about tossing her out,” yelled Fross, sitting in his bed again.

“She shot you twice,” his second-in-command pointed out.

“It was an honest mistake,” protested Fross. “She didn’t understand what was happening. I’ll make everything better tomorrow.”

His friend left him as Fross fell asleep to heal.

Sarang

Fross woke up to see his friends surrounding him. *This isn't going to be good*, he thought. And, sure enough, the conversation was not one he would put into his fond memories.

"You must get rid of her, Fross," Kogu began, his amber eyes full of silver. "She is a danger both to you and to the rest of us."

"He is right, Fross, and you know it," Alaistair agreed, concern showing in his eyes. "She has her bodyguard here now. She will be fine with him."

"What about the curse?" asked Fross, feeling more than a little irritated. "She is the one. I know it."

"Is your life worth lifting that curse?" asked Kogu incredulously. "Will you even be alive if the curse is lifted? It is too dangerous."

Fross sighed and wiped the remaining tiredness out of his eyes. *This could go on for hours if I let it*, he thought. He looked toward his friends and realized that Paola hadn't said anything.

"What are your thoughts on this silly idea, Paola?" Fross asked, throwing her into it.

She looked at him with a bit of a startled look. Her hand reached for her pink locks and began to twist them around her finger much as Ash did.

"She needs time to adjust," Paola finally said. "She was ripped from her family and brought here after seeing much violence."

Fross nodded, thinking about the assassination in which more people were killed by friendly swords than by enemies'.

"Are you saying that last night could have been triggered by something she saw?" asked Kogu, still incredulous.

Paola nodded. "It was most likely something she heard or saw."

Alaistair spoke. "Then it would be better to keep her here rather than out there where she could become a chance informant for one of our enemies."

Fross nodded, secretly relieved. "It is settled. She stays."

* * * * * *

Fross paced the room, the carpeted floor softening the sound of his feet. He looked at the clock, it had been five minutes since he looked last. He grunted time moved too slow for him.

The door to the adjoining room opened and Paola stepped out.

"She is awake."

Fross began to rush to the door but Paola put her hand on his arm.

"Be careful in what you say, she has the fire to your icy demeanour."

With that, Paola let him through and left the room.

Fross walked into the room and saw Ash lying in her bed with pillows to prop her up.

Ash stiffened when she saw Fross enter the room.

"How are you already up?" she asked, curiosity flooding her. "I shot you twice. That would put most humans in the ground."

He stopped and looked at her with some hesitation.

"I am a little bit different than most humans," he began, rubbing the back of his neck. "But it doesn't matter at the moment."

Ash sighed in frustration. *How am I supposed to verify the truth of the man's words if I can't get Fross to open up about his past?* she thought, thinking about the man with the green eyes in the dream last night. *I refuse to believe I just made that all up. It wasn't just a dream.*

"How are you doing?"

The question caught Ash off guard since she was still in her own thoughts.

"What?" she asked, thinking she had heard him wrong.

Fross smiled and sat on the edge of her bed.

"How are you doing?" he repeated, looking slightly concerned.

"I'm fine now," Ash said, trying to nudge Fross off the bed with her leg. He ignored her.

"Splendid. I wondered if Alaistair had given you some brain damage; he punches quite hard."

"Yes," Ash winced, remembering the seconds before she blacked out. "He does."

Fross patted her hand and smiled.

"I was hoping you would like to join me later for a walk, say around mid-afternoon?" he asked, eyes glowing with hope.

Ash looked at him for a couple of seconds and then said, "Yes, that sounds like a good idea."

"Wonderful!" exclaimed Fross. He left the room, feeling lighter than he had in many years. *Today is the day I ask her*, he thought.

Ash rested on the pillows and looked up to the ceiling. *Today is the day I find out what is happening here. No more secrets.*

******

The rest of the day went quickly and soon Ash was on her way to meet Fross at the garden gate. Paola, being the ever-helpful elf, brought her there after having changed Ash into a light-rose dress with a single pearl on a pendant and some sturdy-but-fashionable shoes. Once at the gate, Paola squeezed Ash in a quick hug and bounded off, smiling.

Shaking her head at her friend's silly behaviour, Ash turned to see Fross dressed in a suit of forest green and a cravat that had the lightest hints of pink amid the forest green. Fross bowed to her silently and, playing along, Ash curtsied. Then, still without a sound, Fross took her hand and led her through the gate.

As they walked in silence on the path, Fross began to fidget with his cravat. Noticing this, Ash asked: "Is it too tight?"

Fross stopped fidgeting.

"No, it is fine."

Ash thought it was a strange answer, which raised her suspicions. She looked and saw a small covered patio in the distance.

"Let's go over there," she said, pointing at the structure.

"You read my mind," Fross said, with a glow in his eyes.

They quickly walked over and sat down. Fross went back to fidgeting with his cravat and, after a minute or two, Ash couldn't take it anymore.

"Now it is just getting annoying," she announced and walked over to where Fross was sitting in a wooden chair. She bent down at the waist and began to undo the knot holding the cravat on his neck.

Fross stiffened as she did this. Soon the cravat was off and Ash was holding it.

"There," she said, as she began to straighten her back. Her eyes met Fross's and were mesmerized by them once again. She stared at them for a while but realized her proximity to him and quickly backed away and sat down, blushing.

Fross cleared his throat and began to speak.

"Since I met you, Ash—" He whispered her name as if it was too good to say, making her head whip up and look at him. "I have been drawn to you. You are a beauty and very stubborn, two characteristics I like very much about you." He licked his lips as if he was nervous. "You are not afraid of your strength and don't act like how ladies are trained to act. You are also caring and have a certain aura around you that draws me in." He came closer and grasped her hands in his own and bent down on one knee. "I can't stop thinking about you and have come to believe that I love you."

Ash gasped. *He can't love me, he has killed more than one of us who serve the Creator.* She stood up and looked him straight in the eye.

"Lord Arcop," she began, "you can never love me. I serve the Creator and you kill those who do so, and there is no way that I could love you since you do such vile things."

Fross stood up, his brown eyes flashing cold.

"That is not true, I have never killed those who serve the Creator, but I do know that I love you," he said.

"Lying isn't a good look for you, so leave it be," Ash stated, voice trembling. She ripped her hands out of his and ran, not caring where she ended up.

Fross watched her go and felt a single tear fall from his eye. He turned and stormed back to the house.

"Give her time, Fross," Paola said, appearing from the shadows. "I have reason to believe she does care for you."

"Do you also have reason to believe she serves the Creator?" Fross asked. Paola startled at the question. "She is one of them! How could I be so stupid to fall for it?"

"Well, maybe she is the one who will show you the way," Paola counselled, as was her job. "Maybe it is time to submit to Him and then she might fall in love with you. The truth will always set you free."

"Even if it makes you a monster?" Fross yelled over his shoulder as he stalked away to find someone to spar with.

He went to his desk after finding no one to spar with. *I did everything He said to do but still, I'm stuck here. Can she love me? Or am I too old for such thoughts?* He looked to the ceiling and, for the first time in a long time, prayed.

Numinous

Ash's lungs screamed as they burned for oxygen. Her legs began to wobble but she kept going onward in the rose dress she'd worn to meet Fross. It was hiked up past her knees as she ran as if from a forest fire. Finally, she bent down, letting her dress go and putting her hands on her knees, panting and gasping for breath. She looked up, saw oaks and maples creating a canopy above her, and smiled. She was at home. Ash saw a trail and followed it, walking. Inhaling, she smelled the freshness from the rain the night before and began to put a bounce in her step, something she hadn't done since she'd learned about the wedding. Her smile dwindled when she thought about Fross and the heartbroken look he'd given her. *He was just pretending the entire time, don't worry about him*, she thought, but she couldn't get rid of the guilty feeling that she had had an effect on him that was more than platonic. She shook her head, dismissing the fact, and continued on the path that soon opened to a large field. *Had it only been a little less than two weeks since I ran into the forest?* She wondered at the thought as she made her way up to the castle. It didn't look so bad from the edge of the forest.

She went to the front gate. It was mangled and burnt. Seeing this, Ash ran through the castle and to the throne room. There was no preparation for what she saw. Though someone had tried to clean up after the bodies, the floor was stained a blood red and blood was spattered on all the decorations and walls.

Ash covered her mouth and ran up to the quarters of her old room. The wooden door had been broken down and it looked like there had been a fire in her room. However, all the furniture was still intact. Ash fell to the floor as the tears fell in torrents, covering her dress.

She sat there for she didn't know how long, sobbing and letting all the memories of her old life surface; saying goodbye to each of them. She got up and walked to the bathroom that was surprisingly undamaged and intact. She gripped the rim of the porcelain sink and tried to steady her hands.

"Let me see them, one last time," she whispered to herself. "One. Last. Time."

Ash relived her tumultuous childhood, remembering all the times she was with one of her parents—the good times, the bad times and the terrible times. Her eyes began to ache from crying but Ash wasn't done. She let herself drown in self-pity and tears as she remembered her current predicament.

I can't stay away from him forever; he would find me wherever I go, she told herself, slowly standing up from where she had collapsed in front of her old sink. She washed her hands, remembering when there had been blood in the water as it went down the sink. "But for now, I will stay away from him."

Ash, now refreshed from her breakdown but still with a cracked and bruised heart from the events of the last two weeks, picked her way back down through the destroyed castle to the gate.

She was in the front hall when she slipped on some rubble, falling and hitting her head. Her vision began to tunnel and Ash thought she was going to black out, but the tunnel vision receded and she gingerly got to a seated position, trying to keep her tears at bay as she checked herself for scrapes. She touched her head and saw bright red as she brought her hand to her eyes. Ash checked again and felt that she had a considerable gash on her head, but she couldn't feel it at all. *Maybe I'm too numb to function properly*, she thought absently.

There was a crunch of gravel and a familiar voice floated through the air.

"Are you all right, madame?" the silky voice asked.

Ash turned to see a tall man in a dark-blue jacket and pants picking his way to her. He stopped in front of her and took a bow.

"Verd Winfield, at your service, Miss . . . ?" His eyebrows were raised in silent question as he extended his hand to her.

She took his hand and rose to her feet, replying, "Etton, Ash Etton."

His eyebrows returned to place as a full malice twinkled in his green eyes.

"Ash Etton," he purred. "What a lovely name for such an exquisite lady."

Ash blushed at his tone.

"Well, Mr. Winfield, I do suppose I should thank you for helping me," she said, walking with the man while remembering her long lessons in etiquette with her mother. "Thank you, kind sir, I am in your debt for guiding me out of this castle."

He nodded his head and Ash caught his scent on the slight breeze, reminding her of the dreams to which she had been subjected, but she thought nothing of it as the enchanting man began to speak again now that they were outside of the ruined castle.

"My pleasure, my love." He spoke in a rolling but silky accent. "If you would be so kind as to have a spot of food with me, you would lift my spirits up so much."

Ash thought about it and agreed to it. *Nothing bad could happen from eating with this nice man*, she thought.

Suddenly there was a carriage driven by coal-black horses and the man helped her into the carriage. He closed the door and began to talk to her once again and regale her with tales of his youth.

* * * * * *

They ended up going to a small tavern in a small town, the name of which Ash couldn't ever remember how to pronounce. The tavern, called The Next Castle, was filled with very warm and cottage-like scents that warmed Ash to the core.

"What would you like to dine on tonight, young couple?" asked an elderly lady with dulled-red curls pulled back in a ponytail.

"Oh, we are just friends," explained Ash, seated across from Verd in the small nook to which they had been shown.

The lady just looked at her with tired eyes and an old smile.

"Whatever you say, honey." She looked toward Verd and her eyes widened like saucers. Verd stared at her with indignation covering his face.

"Don't you have something to say to her," Verd leaned close enough to see the lady's name card, "Annabelle?"

The server turned to Ash and completed a low curtsy that Ash was sure pained her to do.

"Forgive me, my lady, I meant no disrespect." The lady straightened at Verd's behest and quickly ran back to get what Verd had said: "The best the tavern can offer."

Ash looked toward Verd, seeing a smile that sent shivers down her back.

"Did you have to be so rude and scare her?" Ash asked, taken aback at the dangerous look in his eyes. "She was just doing her job. Who are we to be so snobby to her?"

"Well, Ash Etton," he rolled her mother's maiden name strangely on his tongue, focusing his glowing eyes on her, "no one is allowed to scoff at me or my associates. I own this town, so those within the town know the consequences of crossing me." His eyes glowed with evil as he said these words.

Ash had begun to stand up when the lady came back with their food, casting a frightened look at Ash. Ash sat back down knowing that if she left Annabelle would probably be hurt. She looked toward the stew that was in front of her.

"Does it please you or should I take someone's ear or finger for displeasing you, my love?" Verd asked smoothly, as if discussing the weather and nothing more.

"It is fine, Verd," said Ash, hoping the use of his name would satiate him. It did and he began to eat. Ash picked at her food. *Fross would never act like this.* The thought popped into her head but it was like she had said it out loud.

Verd's spoon stopped scraping against the wooden bowl and there was a terrible hush that fell over the table.

"If that is how you feel," he began, looking stormy, "then I shall leave you."

Verd grabbed his jacket and left, leaving Ash with the bill.

She began to shake from fear of the beautiful-but-dangerous man and what he was capable of. Ash rested her head on the table and her vision tunnelled again.

* * * * * *

"Ash! Wake up!"

Ash felt a hand shake her roughly and bolted upright, fearing the worst. But she was met with mismatched brown eyes full of concern.

She pushed back her betrothed and escaped into the waiting arms of Paola. Ash looked for Gill in the tavern but saw no trace of him.

"He is at the castle looking for other traces of you and the Black Eagles," said Paola, as if reading her mind.

Ash stepped back, nodding, and saw Alaistair and Kogu watching with worried faces.

"What happened, Shadowwalker?" asked Fross, tapping her shoulder.

"I went out," Ash said honestly. "Am I not allowed to do that?"

There was a harsh hiss from Fross.

"Of course, but who were you with?"

The question froze Ash inside.

"Does it matter?" she asked. She numbly walked out of the door and into the carriage as the sky began to grumble with its burden of rain.

The rain had coated everything by the time they had gotten back to Arcop Manor. Ash didn't care and ran to her room and locked the door. She flung herself onto her bed and ignored the knocking from Fross and Paola and, once, even from Kogu.

La Douleur Exquise

The morning began with Ash waking up to an earsplitting crack. She grabbed her knife and crept to the door, not bothering with a privacy robe since she had never changed out of the dress from the day before. She heard another crack, just as earsplitting as the first, and crouched down further as heavy footsteps came into the room.

Ash inhaled and rounded the corner, knife raised, to see Alaistair. She huffed and rested the knife at her hip.

"What are you doing in here?" She looked past him to see the remnants of her door. "And what did you do to my door?"

Alaistair shrugged at the door.

"It can be fixed," he rumbled. "But you can't stay in this room, you don't know how much you mean to Fross."

"Well, he should have thought of that before slaughtering hundreds of servants of the Creator," she bit back.

Alaistair looked surprised.

"He never did that, Ash. He was only framed for it." His golden eyes fixed on hers. "Please, Ash, Fross needs you. We all do."

Ash sighed.

"Does Fross know how good a friend he has in you?" she asked rhetorically, as he shook his head. She thought for a few seconds and then decided. "All right, when he learns what love is, then I'll talk to him."

Alaistair's hopeful face fell.

"He has had 200 years on the dot of your wedding day to learn how to love and he has yet to do so. Please, come and teach him," Alaistair begged. "He won't listen to us on such matters."

Ash relented slightly.

"All right, I will see him, just not today or anytime soon. I need time to think and to mourn. After all, he has done nothing wrong for me to act so terribly toward him." Ash turned around and walked into her more private bedroom area and closed the doors there. She sat down at the small writing table where the Book of the Creator was hidden. She opened the leather binding and began to read it.

******

A few hours passed and Ash would not let anyone into her rooms. Her outer door was fixed and she locked it. Then she unlocked the interior door and opened her windows to let in the midday light. Soon enough, there was a light knock.

"Ash?" A southern voice spoke. "It's me, Paola. Please let me in, chica."

Ash relented and let in her elf friend who came in laden with a giant basket of food. Once she was in, Ash relocked the door.

"Don't worry, he won't come in. He is stuck in his library, thanks to Alaistair," Paola said, referring to Fross or he-whose-name-will-not-be-said.

Ash smiled and returned to the Book. Paola came into the room and saw it.

"What is it about?" asked the she-elf. "They say it is treasonous writing but I don't think that is true."

"Would you like me to read some to you?" asked Ash, looking up from the Book. Paola nodded, making Ash smile, and she began to read to her friend who was sitting cross-legged on the floor.

After a while there was a knock at the new door. Paola hurried and disappeared around the corner. She returned with a large bouquet of flowers and other small gifts of gold and jewels.

"Looks like someone is begging," mused Paola as she showed the things to Ash.

Ash sighed and turned away from the things.

"Could I send them back?" she asked.

"You could, but do you really want to? These are some of the family jewels," Paola observed.

Ash steeled herself and locked eyes with her friend.

"Yes, I do."

And that was that. The jewels were sent back to Fross. Only the bouquet was kept, due to the fact that it was comprised of white roses.

Ash kept her door locked and only let in select visitors, such as the trio of warriors, whom she had grown to love as friends, and Gill. When Paola came, she and Ash would talk about the Creator, among other things, but never broached the topic of Fross.

Ash was at peace, and happy that she could have a few days away from that man, even though her treacherous heart sometimes longed for him.

* * * * * *

Fross sighed. It had been a week since he had professed his love for her and everything had fallen apart. He was in his library, like most days since the incident, reading a partial copy of the Book, which Paola had swiped from Ash's old room in Cartier Castle. He wondered what had happened in that castle that had made Ash so broken.

Fross got up and walked down to her room and stood there. He thought about all of the gifts he'd sent her to ask for forgiveness. A smile tugged at his lips as he glanced at the new door that Laura, the manor's engineer, had created in record time. No amount of money or jewels could woo Ash. Maybe that's what he liked best about her, but Fross was still unsure.

"It's now or never," Fross told himself, and raised his hand. He knocked on the door three times, his heart pounding louder with every knock.

The door opened and a green head popped out. Paola, of course. She looked at him as if studying him for a second and then nodded.

"It's time you two talk," she said sagely and went back into the room, leaving the door open for him.

Fross walked in and saw Ash looking like a ray of light in the darkened room. *Keep yourself together.* He cleared his throat and glanced at Ash, seeing her guarded expression. *Who made her so suspicious? I'll kill him before I let him hurt her again.*

"Would you spend tomorrow with me, Shadowwalker?" he asked, bowing. His mismatched eyes begging.

Ash closed her eyes and for a second it seemed like she was listening to someone else. Her eyes opened again, showing her azure pools. She smiled the slightest smile and locked eyes with him.

"Yes, I will, Slayer," she said, her smile leaving her face at the mention of his title.

Fross's heart began to pound again and he fought the arrogant smile that wanted to take over his face.

"I'll see you at breakfast, then." He bowed and left the room, now curious about the rest of the Book he was reading. While lost in thought, Fross almost bumped into Gill in the hallway outside of Ash's room.

"Nice sword you have there," the tracker said to Fross.

Fross glanced down at his knightfall, a sword that had kept him company these past 219 years.

"Thank you," Fross replied, trying to keep his tone light. "Yours looks dangerous as well."

Gill grinned, not in a friendly way but rather like a predator who had cornered his prey.

"It has seen over fifty kills. How about yours?" Gill's eyes narrowed with suspicion as he asked the question.

Fross began to answer, only to be interrupted when Paola popped her head out again and clicked her tongue at them disapprovingly. She motioned for Fross to move along while telling Gill that Ash was ready to see him. Fross kept his gaze friendly while Gill gave him a stormy stare, as if it was his fault Ash was like this. *Maybe I am part of the reason.* Guilt seeped into him as he walked back to his library.

I'll make it better, he promised himself, *even if I have to move the world to do so.*

Fross entered his library and went about making plans for the things they would do together the next day, forgetting about the Book entirely.

It was late when he finished, content with the next day's agenda. At that moment, Alaistair came in.

"What is this?" asked the giant.

"These are the plans for tomorrow," Fross responded giddily.

The giant looked at what he had written and walked over to the fireplace that Fross enjoyed having lit even though all their lighting was electric. He looked at the plans for a few more minutes and then threw them into the blaze.

"What are you doing?!" yelled Fross at the giant. "You can be such a brute!"

Alaistair shrugged.

"That isn't the way you woo a girl like Ash," he pointed out. "She isn't fazed by riches or material goods."

Fross crossed his arms. "Well, what is she into then?" he asked sarcastically. "Since you know her oh-so well."

Alaistair looked at his friend with eternal patience.

"Have you read that entire copy yet?" he asked, pointing at the sheaf of papers—Ash's handwritten copy of the Book—resting on a very cluttered table.

"Of course not, it is confusing and seems to contradict itself at multiple points," Fross grumbled, not wanting to show weakness to his friend. Alaistair shook his head, surprising his friend. "Oh, so you've been listening to her talk about Him too? Paola was bad enough," Fross huffed.

"It is the way to connect with her and, if I remember correctly, you asked her to talk about the Creator when you were sick," Alaistair observed, lifting his eyebrows.

"That was in a moment of weakness," said Fross.

"If you say so, boss." Alaistair never called him that unless he wanted Fross to really listen to him. "But if I were you, I'd read the rest of the copy. I wouldn't want to lose her to someone else."

Fross's head snapped up.

"Kogu would never and neither would you. Paola would have your head if you tried."

"You are correct about that, but what about Gill?" asked the giant quietly. "You haven't been seeing his glances recently. They are more than platonic. Be careful in what you say."

With that, the giant left. Fross glanced at the Book and, after a few minutes, let his need overcome his arrogance and blind pride. He picked up the Book and began to read from where he had left off.

It was past midnight when he finished and went to sleep. *Good thing I decided to have a light breakfast at mid-morning rather than an early, large one.*

NAZ

The day began with clouds that were quickly chased away by cheery sunlight before breakfast. Ash woke up early, as was her way, remembering what the day had in store. *A full day with Fross.* The thought gave her feelings of joy and excitement as well as of apprehension. She had just sat up in her bed when she was surprised by Paola, who had been sitting in the corner waiting for her to wake up.

"Good morning!" she chirped, jumping onto the bed. "Get up, silly! We have to get you ready for today."

Not given time to answer, the elf pulled Ash out of bed and took her into the bathroom where a bath had been drawn and was waiting for her.

"Go and begin to bathe," the elf ordered as she rifled through the large closet that held clothes from ballroom dresses to swimsuits. "I'll do your hair in a few minutes."

Ash did as she was told and groaned in pleasure as the heat of the water enveloped her. She normally only had a quick shower, for speed and to use less water, but the occasional bath was quite lovely too. She looked toward the baskets of flowers, soaps, and bath milk. After a few minutes of smelling the scents, she decided on a rose-petal bath with hints of vanilla and sandalwood. She bathed in luxury, scrubbing her arms and legs to a clean pink. Ash wasn't worried about germs but something told her that she should try to look more put-together than usual. Her heart began to pound as she thought about Fross. *Is this what it is like to court someone?* she wondered as she once again lathered her exfoliant sponge. She had gotten into the idea that using an exfoliant sponge and then a smoother and softer sponge would help keep her skin calm. To her surprise, it worked and helped to cleanse her better.

There was a tap on her shoulder and Ash twisted her head to see violet eyes.

"Hair?" Paola reminded her.

Ash nodded, pulled her wet braid out of the bathwater to hand it to the elf, and went back to scrubbing herself. The elf made quick work of the braid, undoing it and combing out the tresses. Ash scooted forward to give Paola space to clean her hip-length brown hair. Paola poured new warm water on her hair and was quickly scrubbing and massaging the hair and scalp with rose-scented soap. The two of them worked in comfortable silence with only the swish of water filling the air.

Finally, after what seemed to be an eternity, Ash was ready for the next step in this fun process. Paola left for a few minutes to let Ash get out of the tub and dry off. She put on matching underwear for the second time in her life, the first being at her wedding. *The wedding.* Ash sighed. She wished she could redo it and make it more memorable for the right reasons.

Paola returned with an armful of lotions and a small bag of makeup. Seeing her friend's grimace when Ash saw the bag, she set it aside.

"Don't worry, chica. I won't force you to wear it," said Paola, calming the worry she saw on Ash's face.

Ash smiled in thanks and sat down at the armoire and looked at the different creams the elf had brought.

"Umm . . ." she paused, unsure how to continue. "Which ones go where?"

Paola gave her a bright smile, which made the elf's violet eyes twinkle, and quickly explained the lotions.

Soon, the process was finished and it was time for the dress. Ash was brought out into the bedroom, where a lovely white dress with red trim and embroidery lay on the bed. Ash slid into the dress that flowed around her body, not showing off her body but also not hiding her curves. It hit her around the knees and hung from her shoulders with thick straps. Paola gave her a shawl of the same pattern and sprayed her with vanilla-and-rose scent.

"Just perfect!" she exclaimed, looking a little bit teary-eyed.

"Thank you, Paola!" squeaked Ash as she looked into the mirror. She did look wonderful. "Is Fross coming to take me to breakfast or should I go there to meet him?"

Paola scoffed. "He is old-fashioned, still stuck 200 years in the past. Alaistair will accompany you to the room."

Ash looked at the clock on the wall. He should be here any minute now. She checked her hair: the twisted crown similar to the hairstyle from her wedding, but now with white ribbons and hair floating freely down her back. There was a knock at the door and Ash's heart picked up in tempo.

It is showtime, she told her mirrored reflection, and walked over to open the door.

Alaistair was at the door, a smile creasing his face as he saw Ash.

"My lady." He held out his arm and Ash took it, smiling back at Paola as the giant guided her to the breakfast.

They were almost there when Alaistair spoke up. "Thank you for agreeing to this. We all really needed it. And don't worry about what Fross thinks about your dress."

This caused Ash to stop. "How did you . . . ?"

"It was written all over your face. Fross hired me to read people and let's just say I have had a lot of practice," Alaistair explained as they reached the wooden doors to the room where Fross and Ash had had their first dinner together a few weeks ago. "Have a good time," Alaistar said as he opened the door.

Within the room, Fross stood and was fidgeting with his cravat once again. This time it was the same red as her dress. Alaistair deposited Ash inside the room and left, closing the doors behind him.

Ash looked toward Fross bashfully, new feelings stirring within herself. He looked just as nervous.

"Should we sit down?" she prodded him gently.

"Yes, of course," he said, trying to recapture his pride. But it was all he could do to not gawk at her. She was a vision to him.

Ash looked at the dish placement and saw they were at opposite ends of the table once more. She looked at Fross with a twinkle in her eye and picked up her dishes, making slight clinking noises as she placed them into a manageable stack. She placed them to the right of where Fross sat and plopped down in the chair, looking at Fross with a grin. Fross grinned back, showing his dimples.

The breakfast went quickly as they talked about sparring. They joked with each other, laughing more at their laughs than at the actual jokes. They ate their fill of food and went out to the garden that they had gone to a week ago.

It seemed that Fross wanted to cover old memories with better ones. He once again led her to the pavilion, but this time he seated her on the loveseat and sat beside her.

"No declarations of love. I just want to talk to a lovely lady that outshines the garden in every way," Fross informed Ash, as some pink coloured his cheeks.

Ash smiled. "No declarations of love," she agreed, turning her body to better see him.

Fross smiled and looked out at the garden.

"I love being out here." He almost whispered. "It was my favourite spot as a child, but back then it did look quite different. There were oaks in here and some more lilac bushes that died out. They were my mother's favourite."

Ash grabbed his hand with her ballroom gloves. "They were my grandmother's favourite too," she said, squeezing his hand gently.

His gaze shot to her gloves.

"Why do you wear the gloves?" he asked quietly.

Ash pulled her hand away from his grasp and sighed sadly. She looked into his eyes.

"Are you sure you want to hear this?" she asked timidly.

He nodded, heart pounding.

Ash looked into his gaze as she began.

"Before I start this story, I must tell you something else that you might find to be sad and disturbing." She paused, looking for hesitation. She found none and continued. "I am a servant of the Creator."

Ash's gaze slipped from Fross's. He took a finger and gently brought her gaze to meet his once again.

"I know you are. It doesn't bother me anymore," he said in an intimate voice.

Ash nodded. Fross took his finger from under her chin and took her hand.

Ash continued and kept her gaze focused on Fross's beautiful, mismatched eyes. Her own eyes held the shimmer of tears.

"I learned about Him from an old man in the market who gave me a copy of the Book. I would sometimes talk to him when I could get away from the castle, which became harder as the years went by. One day, though, when I was seven, I was caught talking to him about a passage that was very difficult to understand. He was instantly thrown into the dungeon and I was sent to my father, the head elder of our little clan from the southwest. I was ready for any type of punishment—whipping, extra chores, anything." Her gaze slid back down to her hand that was entwined with Fross's, and she clenched her free hand.

"I was sent to my room without lunch and dinner but I wasn't ready for what happened next. The next day, I was brought from my room and taken to the open courtyard. I was given a sword and set in front of the prisoner I was supposed to execute. They took off the hood covering the person's head and it was—" She inhaled a shaking breath as a tear escaped her cheek. Fross wanted to wipe it away but didn't want to disturb the story. She continued. "It was my teacher, the old man. He had been beaten badly, his eyes almost totally swollen shut, and it looked like his jaw had been partially dislocated. He turned his head toward me, sensing my hesitation. He said, 'My child, my time has come. The Creator calls me home. He will give you the strength to continue. He will always be with you, Ash.' I couldn't do it. My father tried to get me to kill him by insulting me and even whipping me, but I refused. I would have rather died than take my teacher's life. Finally, my father had enough of my refusal and commanded one of the guards to help me do it. He grabbed my hands and forced the sword hilt between them and, using his strength, swept the sword down upon my teacher's neck as he smiled encouragingly at me. It took him three tries to totally sever his head." Her voice cracked and she paused, regrouping. "Which I think was part of my father's punishment."

"But my punishment wasn't finished," she said calmly. "As soon as the execution was finished—it was my first time at one of those—I was whisked away to my father's office again, my teacher's blood still covering me. Once there, my father, along with the other elders, made me watch as they threw a copy of the Book, which I had finished the week before, into the fire. I screamed and rushed toward the fire but was unwilling to put in my hands to save the pages. My mother, who had decided to watch, took my hands and stuck them in the fire. She laughed as I screamed from the agony. Once she was satisfied, my mother left, leaving me to my own devices. There was a servant who took pity on me and brought a bowl of water to douse my hands. She took me to my room and protected me from my parents, at the cost of her own life. She was a servant of the Creator and was executed the next day, with me watching."

Ash blinked away the tears as best she could. "I can still see the blood from both me and my teacher running down the sink. The Creator took mercy on me and gave me the use of my hands, even though the scars remain."

Fross felt ready to burst with rage. *Who would want to do something so terrible?* The thought was answered by another one: *You would.* He knew it was the truth and felt disgusted with his old actions. *I can't keep living like this. It is wrong.* He looked at Ash, who was silently staring at her gloved hands. *Maybe it isn't too late.*

He took both of her hands. "Ash," he said softly. She raised her head and he saw her pools of azure flooding down her pink, tear-stained cheeks.

"Can I . . . is it too late?" He paused, trying to find the best words, but gave up his search. "I want to become like you." Seeing her confusion, he continued wiping the tears as they exited her eyes. "I want to be a servant of the Creator. I don't know if my friends would be so happy to hear this, but I know this is the right thing to do."

She stared at him surprised. "Are you sure? It won't be an easy life," she warned.

He squeezed her hands. "I have never been so sure of anything in my entire life," he stated, smiling.

"Well, the easiest way to do it is to simply ask Him," she said with a smile gracing her lips.

"Do I have to do anything special?" he asked, unsure.

She shook her head. "I can pray with you if you want." He agreed and she began, with him following along. "Dear Creator, I ask you to become the guide of my life and I give over the control of my life. I know you died to save me and to give me a way to live with you forever. Please give me this life as I live for you until the day I die and see you."

They stopped and Ash looked at Fross, tears blocking her vision. She felt him wipe away the tears.

"Why do you cry, Ash?" he asked, choking on his own tears of joy.

"I'm so very happy," she sobbed. "I wanted you to become a servant of the Creator since before I met you."

The tears began to spill from Fross's eyes and he placed their heads together, forehead to forehead, and let the tears mingle down together. They stayed like that for a very long time, crying with each other.

Finally, the tears stopped, and Ash regarded her betrothed in a new light. He seemed to glow from the inside out, his caramel skin becoming more healthy-looking than it had before. He pulled out a red handkerchief and gave it to her. She saw the monogram on it, making it his.

"You can keep it if you want," he said in a soft voice. He paused as if hesitating. "Could I see your hands?"

She nodded and began to unbutton and pull off the red, white-trimmed, shoulder-length gloves. They slowly came off, inch by inch, exposing pale skin full of jagged white lines. Fross guessed that her body would be littered with scars from her old hunting trips, as well as being a living tapestry that reflected fights and near-misses with death. Whether accidental or not, Fross didn't know. He knew one thing, though: She was the most beautiful creature the Creator had ever made.

Ash paused when she reached her wrists. Her eyes flickered to Fross's, which were full of encouragement and love. She sucked in a breath and, with shaky hands, she pulled off her left glove and then her right one in quick succession. It was Fross's time to gasp. Her hands were completely white, with what looked to be flames licking at the edge of her wrist like a frozen fire. Other than that, her hands didn't seem to be damaged, with no parts of melted skin or anything.

Fross gently took her hands and looked up at her.

"Can you feel anything in your hands?" he asked.

She nodded. "He was gracious in the healing."

Fross began to bring up her hands to his face, but, feeling her began to stiffen with fear, he bent his head down and pressed chaste kisses—one on each of the backs of her hands and one on each of her palms. Her breath hitched and she became still.

Fross looked back up at her. "I'm sorry these things happened to you. Had I known . . ." He paused. "Back then I would have had a laugh along with your parents, but now I would slaughter them myself." His rage was becoming unchecked and Fross desperately tried to regain control. "But even that wouldn't be right. It would be right to let the Creator deal with them."

Ash nodded. She slipped one of her hands out of his and cradled the side of his face. "It isn't for us to take revenge, but rather to show love."

This confused Fross.

"But to love like that wouldn't be wrong? I thought that was for a couple."

Ash laughed a beautiful, full laugh.

"Not that type of love, Fross. Neighbourly love and the love of friends. There are more types of love than just between the sheets or between a man and a woman. True love is not romantic, as many people think, but rather what the Creator gave to us. He died for those who hated him. That is true love," Ash explained, a smile brightening her face.

Fross touched her shoulder in a way both friendly and confiding.

"You don't have to wear the gloves around me. In fact, I would rather you didn't." His cheeks glowed slightly pink. "You look wonderful without them."

Ash blushed and Fross went back to playing with his cravat again. Ash leaned in close to Fross and undid the cravat, pulling it away from his neck. She stood up, with a playful look crossing her face.

"Catch me!" was all she said as she danced away from the pavilion that they had been sitting in for a few hours.

Fross's heart quickened as he watched her run away, dancing in a way that put the butterflies to shame. She seemed to be lighter than air as she nimbly floated through the garden. He stood up and ran after her, laughing in a way that he hadn't for over a century.

He caught her in a field after a few minutes of her dancing away from his grasp, teasing him, and leading him away from the garden and the manor.

"Got you!" he announced, grabbing her waist. For a few minutes he felt like any other twenty-year-old running after the girl of his dreams. She squealed as he began to tickle her. Soon enough, they fell to the ground laughing, out of breath.

Fross rolled on top of Ash, keeping his weight on his arms on either side of her head. Her shawl had come undone and had fluttered to a resting position on a bush a few steps away. He saw more of the white scars covering her shoulders and around her collarbone.

"They were very demanding that I stop believing in such nonsense," Ash explained lazily, all memories of her past far away from her mind as she was captivated by the young man on top of her. "You were the latest option, a way to sweep their embarrassment of a daughter under the rug."

Fross was taken aback.

"I didn't know you were opposed to the arrangement until it was too late," he said regretfully. "I only began to wonder when you hesitated."

He leaned down and gave Ash a quick kiss on her lips. Rolling to his side, he propped himself on his elbow.

"That is my apology." He gave her a rugged but sweet smile.

She returned his smile with one of her own.

"I hope you continue to apologize in that fashion," she said. A deep red blush crept up her face.

Fross laughed, stood up, and helped up Ash, knowing that she could get up on her own if she so desired. They shared a secret smile and enjoyed each other's company outside until the sun began to set. They had a light dinner, laughing with each other, and soon—too soon, in Ash's opinion—she had to go to bed. Fross walked her to her room, kissed her forehead, murmured a 'goodnight' to her, and was gone.

Ash flopped onto her bed and felt giddy from the events of the day, but sleep soon overtook her.

Kilig

Unlike a normal night of sleep for him, Fross saw the light, a type of light he hadn't seen in a little over 200 years.

"Fross," a booming voice said, "you have done well and have followed my commands. As a reward, I grant you and your household the gift of mortality. I will bless you and your children in a multitude of ways and you will live to a good age with your love. As for the men who you seek for the murders of the Cartiers and their household, I will send you the way to find them. But you must destroy all of them, for through you and your household, I will bring their doom upon them."

The voice and the light left as quickly as they had come. Fross opened his eyes and was greeted by daylight. Suddenly, there was the sound of footsteps rushing into the room and Alaistair appeared, looking frightened to the point of panic.

"Hurry, Fross," he said, beckoning his waking friend. "There is something wrong with Ash!"

******

She was falling, falling into a deep, dark abyss. Ash tried to glide to one of the walls but to no avail. She was stuck in the middle. She began to thrash and the scenery changed as she fell softly onto a couch. Ash got up from the ornate furniture to see that she was in a room covered with other grotesque, ornate things. The place creeped her out and she ran for one of the doors. She pulled the brass knob but it was locked. She twisted and turned it but the handle was completely stuck!

The ground rolled beneath her and she fell down onto the grass. She looked up and saw that she was in a forest clearing with a red sky above her. She jumped to her feet and found herself dressed in barely-there clothing that gave her zero protection, lots of movement, and almost no modesty. There was a crackle behind her and she whipped around, getting closer to the ground as Paola had shown her. A tall and sinister figure came into view and Ash quickly spotted a pair of shining green eyes.

"Verd!" she shouted at him as he approached.

"Ah, so you remember me." He bowed sarcastically. "Quite right, Miss Etton. Or is it Mrs. Arcop?

Her breath caught in surprise.

"Don't think I didn't know your identity." He shook his head sadly. "Mrs. Arcop, I have spies everywhere, my love."

"I am not your love, nor am I yet Mrs. Arcop," she spat out defiantly.

"Not yet you aren't," he stated, turning his back to her. "And as for becoming his wife, well, that has yet to be seen."

She took her strike but Verd grabbed her arm with the speed of a cobra and Ash was pushed back.

She fell back on to a bed. She looked around and saw that her clothing had changed into white pyjamas. Ash tried to roll away but was caught by a strong, white arm.

"Don't leave so soon," he purred into her ear. "We are just getting started."

Ash tried to fight his grip but couldn't move as darkness covered her once again.

******

As they ran down the stairs, Alaistair explained the situation to Fross.

"She was found by the guard, Haon, thrashing on her bed, but she was still sleeping. She began to scream and Haon left his brother Noah there while he ran to my room. I saw what was happening and came to you while sending for Chester."

They had reached Ash's room and the healer was already there. Fross looked toward Ash, who had gone still for the time being. Noah began to wipe her head and she thrashed out again, letting out a cry that cut Fross to the quick. He rushed to her side.

"Ash! Come on, dear, wake up! It is just a dream, it isn't real." As she stopped thrashing, he wiped his hand across her forehead, which had broken out in a sweat. There was a jerking motion and his hand was caught by a white one. He turned to see her azure eyes filled with wildness.

"What happened?" he asked, forgetting about their audience. Her next words struck him to the core.

"Verd . . . Winfield," she croaked, as her eyes rolled back and she went unconscious.

Fross stood up and allowed Chester and Blanche to do their work on her. He walked over to Alaistair, who had his arms crossed and was watching everyone.

"Do you want me to find his location?" the giant's voice rumbled in question.

Fross nodded, glancing at the crowd in the room.

"He has always gotten away from you," the giant pointed out.

"It doesn't matter," Fross stated coldly in his leader's voice. "If he is somehow hurting Ash through dreams, I want to know." He paused. "I need the team prepared for a drop tonight. I want to bring along Ash for practice."

Alaistair nodded.

"Where to?"

"The old smithy, The Rare Sword."

Alaistair clapped a large hand on Fross's shoulder.

"You got it, boss. In my opinion, you should keep Ash as close as possible. She is the perfect match for you."

Fross smiled at his friend.

"Thank you. And, trust me, I have only begun to understand her and love her in every way."

Alaistair's eyebrows raised.

"Every way?" he queried.

"Yes," Fross paused slightly, a smile lighting his features. "I became a servant of the Creator and I've never been so full of life and purpose."

Alaistair grunted, cheeks colouring slightly.

"Interesting."

Fross was soon left by himself in Ash's room. Paola assured him that if he needed a break she would take over the watch, but Fross said that he would be fine. He sat down by the bed, holding his love, and spotted a leather book half-hidden under a pillow. He took it out to see that it was the Book. He began to read it but was soon interrupted.

"I think you are a bit too obsessed with me," a soft and delicate voice said to Fross. He looked over to the bed and saw Ash smiling at him. "I mean, waking up to you by my bed is nice, but you do have a castle to run, as well as various other organizations," she teased him.

Fross smiled.

"It is nice to see you up. Now, how would you feel about going on a mission tonight?" he asked.

Her eyes sparked to life.

"What type of mission?"

******

Night had fallen and it was a new moon, giving the group of five warriors, the twin guards, and Onul Jebel easy cover. It was an easy reconnaissance mission to find the location of the main garrison of the Black Eagles.

Fross led the way, with Ash on his tail and the three warriors and guards protecting them from behind. The climb into the window on the second story had been easy, and it seemed to be going splendidly until Onul stumbled on a loose brick. There was a shout from below. They had been spotted by the guards. A firefight ensued. All of the team carried guns and knives except for Ash. She had a bow, a Frost Willow Recurve; a quiver full of arrows; and Ghostwalker, her Cartier dagger. Fross also sported his longsword.

The battle was brutal and intense but also quickly done. Once it was silent, the team moved on to the ground floor. The floor was completely littered with bullets and bullet casings to the point that the team had to pick their way through the mess.

Ash spotted a sheet of paper and ran nimbly and silently over to it, low to the ground in case there were other members of the gang here. She plucked it off the wall and turned on her flashlight to study it. It appeared to be a crude map of Dasica.

Fross came over and grabbed the map, putting it into a pocket in his black pants that seemed to be covered in little pouches.

"Good job," he whispered in her ear. "But don't go running off like that without alerting someone. You almost gave me a heart attack!"

She nodded, understanding. She fell back into step behind Fross as they continued to check for survivors and information in the smithy.

They had just finished checking the last room, in the far back of the building, when another group of the B.E.G. barged in. They were penned in. Ash was the closest to the invaders and shot one in the heart as another of them shot her in the arm.

Ash groaned loudly and bit back a scream as the pain engulfed her arm. She was roughly pulled back by Paola, who deposited her at the back of the room. Ash sat down, feeling dreadfully dizzy. Things began to lose focus and bleared together. She shook her head but that made things even worse and she leaned back on the stone wall that penned them in. *Is this how I die?* she thought, tears gathering at the corners of her eyes. *If I die tonight, I won't go down quietly.* Ash struggled to her feet, clenching her bow as the waves of pain threatened to throw her back down on the ground. She persevered. Another arm dragged her out of the corner.

"Come on, Ash," Fross yelled. "Haon found a way out."

She felt herself being pushed through an opening, although she could barely focus on anything except Fross's voice. Someone else murmured something as Ash felt herself being deposited into a pair of strong arms. She guessed that it was about her wound bleeding out.

"No, no, no! Ash, stay with me!"

Fross's voice seemed distant but Ash murmured, "Yes, Slayer."

There was a sad laugh and she jolted to her senses. She looked to see Fross watching her as they ran to their vehicle. Well, Fross was running and Ash was being held securely to his chest.

"You're safe," he told the brunette in his arms, and Ash, for once in her life, believed that.

Koi No Yokan

The next day was cloudy and felt full of rain when Ash woke up. She grimaced as she sat up, still feeling the wound from the night before even though the healers had done their best. Well, Blanche had taken care of her while Chester had stared at Blanche in awe. Ash wondered if Blanche realized that her teacher had more than a little affection for her, but it wasn't her place to ask such questions. She spotted a small, cream-coloured envelope with elegant script on the bedside table. Ash picked it up and read its contents, her heart racing.

Dear Ash,

I hope you will forgive me for not being there to see you wake up but, as you said before, I do have a castle and several businesses to run. I have gone away for the day to check some of my resources to find out more about the B.E.G. and perhaps about the man who is behind your nightmares. If you are feeling up to it, and if you will have me, perhaps tonight when I return we could go out for a change of scenery and grab a late meal and show. Please try to not cause Kogu too much trouble; I have Paola and Alaistair with me.

Until the next time we meet,

Fross

The letter had been penned in exquisite handwriting. It warmed Ash to see that Fross was able to create such delicate words and that he had taken the time to do so in what must have been a very busy and early morning for him. *I wonder if he got any sleep at all?* Ash shook the thought away. She knew he could take care of himself, but she couldn't help but worry about him.

Ash was determined to not frustrate Kogu that day and quickly bathed and dressed even though she had nothing to do. She smoothed her hair back and was putting it into her usual braid when a knock sounded at the door. Ash opened the door and saw Kogu in a black shirt and blue jeans.

"What a surprise! I didn't think you had anything else besides black in your closet, Kogu," greeted Ash, a smile pulling at her lips. As always, Kogu was not amused. He grumbled something about first impressions, his face going a bit pink.

He walked in and looked around as if he would find a murderer under the low chairs.

"Are you leaving the property today?" he asked, turning back to her.

Ash shook her head.

"No, I don't think so, but I'm not exactly sure where the property line is," she admitted.

He rolled his eyes and waved her over to the window.

"It goes to the mountains," he pointed to the grey peaks in the distance, "to the river," he pointed right, "to the end of the first forest," he pointed left, "and to the edge of town." Kogu backed away from the window, leaving Ash to gape in awe.

"He owns all that?" she asked, not leaving the window.

"Yes, and more, though this is his largest property by acreage," Kogu responded.

Ash turned to him with a spark in her eyes.

"Well, then, I just might do some exploring," she said, to the chagrin of the warrior. But Kogu said nothing and just nodded his head, leaving her to make her own plans for the day.

******

Fross returned in the late afternoon and Ash went out to meet him. They had a quick embrace and Fross said he needed a few minutes to freshen up. Ash went to her friend, who had been watching them with a wise eye.

"So do you think you could care for him?" the elf asked with a happy glint in her eye.

Ash blushed.

"I could see that happening," she responded, trying to sound calm and indifferent. Paola began to laugh and Ash looked at her friend in surprise.

"You are very easy to read, and your heart is pounding a mile a minute," the elf said, wiping tears from her eyes.

"I'm not that easy to read, you just have better hearing than most." Ash pouted as a question formed in her head. "How was your day?"

Paola placed her arm over her friend's shoulders.

"Boy, do I have a tale to tell," she began.

******

Ash leaned back in her chair and sighed. She was full. As Fross had promised, they had gone out for a meal in town, incognito and without guards. The townspeople didn't seem to care who they were—a refreshing respite after the past few weeks of tight security. Unfortunately, Fross had shown up at an inopportune moment for Ash, who had been trying to get Paola to spill about something that had happened earlier that day. Ash hadn't found out and Fross had quickly whisked her away to a cozy inn that promised the best food in the country. The advertisement hadn't been wrong and the food rivalled even Richard's cooking.

"That was a lovely meal, maybe too lovely." She groaned, closing her eyes. Fross laughed at her silliness and she cracked one eyelid open to see his glowing face.

"Yes, I'm a little full myself," he said, eyes full of mirth. He paid for the meal and got up, waited for Ash to rise from her post-eating repose, and took her arm. "Now, on to the show."

They walked up a small hill and sat at the top, looking at the stars that began to peek out one by one.

"I could watch this forever," breathed Ash, encompassed by the beauty of the night sky.

"So could I," Fross agreed, looking up and then turning his head toward her. "As long as you were with me."

Ash smiled at his words and leaned back to lie down on the grass with her hands under her head. She turned to the boy beside her, who was watching the sky with wonder once more. If she was being honest, Ash had grown to like Fross and enjoyed being around him, but that feeling was much different than what she felt around Gill. Gill was comfortable, like an old friend or a brother to her, while Fross could become something more, maybe already was more. *Could I love him?* She didn't have time to contemplate it as Fross pulled her arm.

"Look over there," he directed, pointing to a large field. She saw some people there who were carrying boxes and had a small fire set up.

"What are they doing?" she asked him.

"Just wait and see."

Ash watched as the people set up a little platform and took something out of one of the boxes. There was a whooshing sound and an object from the box flew through the air and exploded into a bright shimmer of colour. Others quickly followed it, lighting the night sky with all sorts of colours and designs.

"Fireworks!" exclaimed Ash, laughing at the sounds they made going through the air.

Fross stood up and looked down at the girl beside him, cheeks rosy from laughing. He felt the small box in his pocket and his hands turned clammy. He reached down and took her hand, bringing her to her feet. Her azure eyes stared in wonder and curiosity at him. *Oh, Creator, give me strength,* he prayed. As he was about to kneel down, a small tune went through the air. Fross groaned: Someone was calling him.

Ash saw a flash of annoyance cross Fross's face as he pulled out the tiny silver phone that had been making the moment-ruining sound. He checked the caller ID. From the serious look on his face, it was something important.

"I'll be back in a second, but this seems to be important," he said, walking away as he accepted the call. "What is it, Alaistair?"

Why could Alaistair be calling? Ash wondered as she returned her attention to the fireworks. She sighed. *Everything seemed fine before we left and Alaistair is second in command. Why couldn't he take care of the place for a few hours?*

There was an exasperated sigh to her left and she stood, turning toward it. The frightened look on Fross's face did not instill her with any hope of salvaging the night.

"We have to go," he said, taking her back to the small carriage they had taken to the hill. "I promise I'll let you see the full display another time."

******

Back at the house, Paola ushered the two of them into the meeting room, where Alaistair and Kogu awaited them.

"What's going on, Alaistair?" Fross asked uneasily, unconsciously reflecting the mood of the room. Ash sat down beside him, holding his caramel hand beneath the table.

Alaistair produced a simple, square letter.

"This was found at our doorstep less than an hour ago," he rumbled, handing it off to Fross, who opened the note, with Ash reading over his shoulder.

WE ARE COMING FOR HER

It read in big, bold letters. The sight of it made Ash go pale and shake. Under that message she saw her initials. It was her old stationery.

Fross wasn't one bit calm. "Move her room to the one beside mine, on the top floor. I am assigning our best guards to protect her," he ordered almost instantly. He turned to Ash, whose eyes were like saucers. "I won't let them take you," he promised, holding her small hands for a second longer. He nodded to Paola, who came forward.

"Come on, chica. Let's go. The boys will take care of themselves." She pulled Ash along with her as they went up the stairs to the room that Fross had indicated. Paola opened the door. "Go and rest. You need to take care of yourself—for Fross's sake, if not your own."

Ash nodded numbly as the she-elf gave her a tight, reassuring hug and she was locked into the room. She walked over and lay on the bed, a thousand thoughts running through her head. She gradually fell asleep while hearing the sound of footsteps coming down the hall. She knew the sound of Fross's footsteps and these weren't his. She tried to rouse herself but, far too late, she realized that she was drugged. The door opened and just as her eyes closed she glimpsed a pair of sturdy black boots.

MIZPAH

Fross leaned over the map that Ash had gotten from the B.E.G. outpost two nights before. He tiredly rubbed his eyes, which were bordered in dark black circles, but there was too much to do to stop and rest. He had to keep her safe. The lines on the page kept blurring; he had already drunk his fourth cup of Richard's condensed coffee. up fortifying the castle while Kogu and Paola had been sent to rest for a few hours.

"How are we doing?" Fross asked, straightening from his position in front of the map. He groaned as his body moved stiffly.

"Half the guardhouse is deployed while the others rest. I sent Noah into town to collect a few extra supplies in case we need to go on the offensive," Alaistair reported.

Fross nodded and looked at his empty mug, considering whether a fifth cup of coffee was in order, but Alaistair picked up the mug and placed it away from his friend with a warning look that said *No more for you.* Fross sighed.

"I know you are worried about Ash. We all are," Alaistair began in a weary voice, "but you shouldn't worry or doubt us. We care for her, too, and Paola has taken quite a shine to the girl." His eyes gleamed as he said the elf's name. "I would feel the same way if someone had threatened my girl."

Fross looked at his friend.

"When did you get so wise, Alaistair?" he asked, lamely teasing the giant, who cracked a grin. "Though your girl—who I have yet to be introduced to—" he sent the giant a joking glance, "has had more years of practice than Ash, I understand the sentiment."

"I am thinking about proposing to Paola soon," Alaistair blurted, cheeks turning pink. "Probably once the curse is broken, which, with Ash being here, won't be long, will it?" He turned to look at his friend as Fross clapped him on the shoulder.

"Well, my friend, I think you should go and propose now." Alaistair did a double take at the sound of his friend's words, his golden eyes growing wide. "The curse has been broken."

"You really mean that?" the giant almost yelled at his friend in his giddiness, but then became serious again. "About last night—I'm sorry about having to call you away from Ash. I knew you were going to ask her, but . . ." The man trailed off, rubbing the back of his neck.

"It is all right, Alaistair." Fross patted his arm. "I will just ask her another time." He turned back to the map. "Now, as for this map—it is very crude, but that shape over there . . ." He pointed to an upside-down U that was surrounded by others of the same shape. "It seems to be a hill. but there isn't any place like that in Dasica. I've checked other maps multiple times, but—nothing."

Alaistair looked over at the map, brow furrowed.

"I don't recognize most of the landmarks on this map," he admitted after studying the map for a few minutes. "Could it be another country?"

Fross shook his head in answer. His vision began to blur again.

"I think I need to sit down," he told his friend, sitting down on the old couch in the corner of the war room. His friend followed him and took a seat, stifling a groan.

"Do you think it is the gang?" Alaistair prodded, slouching on the couch in fatigue.

Fross shook his head.

"No, it isn't their M.O. They would have come in, guns blazing, and taken her by force. Threatening with a note feels like a different person altogether. I don't like not knowing who." Fross held his head in frustration. "Did you get any information on that man Ash talked about? What was his name this time?"

"Verd Winfield," Alaistair supplied. "And there wasn't much on him. He doesn't leave his place much and keeps to himself, or so I'm told."

"You don't trust the informant?"

"He's a spy, a changeling," Alaistair grunted, looking up at the dull ceiling.

Fross nodded. Changelings weren't known for being loyal or trustworthy, but due to their ability to transform into anyone or anything, they were the best spies. Something that had always put Fross on edge, especially now.

"Did you find any way to put pressure on him?" asked Fross, grimacing. He didn't like to hurt others unnecessarily, but Winfield had hurt Ash, which meant war.

The giant sighed before locking eyes with his best friend. "He kept going on about how he wouldn't let Phase die. Makes me think he isn't doing this by his own volition."

"Anyone else?" Fross asked, hopeful. But his hopes were dashed when Alaistair shook his head. "Well, maybe we won't have to worry about him just yet. But I would like to meet him, just in case."

"I'll drop him a line." Alaistair leaned back, resting his head on the old couch.

"Actually, you don't have to," a voice said.

Both men jumped up, instantly alert and scanning the room for intruders but seeing none.

"I come in peace," the voice continued nervously.

"If you come in peace, then show yourself," commanded Fross, fingering his dagger.

There was a slight sound of hesitation, but then a figure slowly materialized from the wall. Alaistair grunted in surprise while Fross held his breath and became as still as stone. The figure stepped into the light, looking surprisingly human-like with his curly black hair and honey-coloured skin, though his eyes flashed the iconic green, reptilian eye that all changelings had. The eyes then turned to a soft dove-grey colour.

The man had stepped closer to Fross and Alaistair when the giant said, "Hold it there!"

The changeling stopped and Fross realized that they were the same height. Fross approached the changeling.

"Why are you here?" he asked the man.

The changeling looked at Fross and then at Alaistair.

"Don't worry, he won't hurt you," Fross assured the changeling, who looked ready to bolt from seeing Alaistair be protective of his friend.

"Yet," rumbled the giant.

The changeling took a deep breath and began.

"My name is Syn," he began. "I am in the employ of Verd Winfield, or at least I was. He is holding my wife, Phase, captive. We were trying to leave his employ when we learned that our first child was on the way. He found out and since then has used that information against me, to make me continue to do his dirty work with my ability to become completely invisible. This started a little over six months ago. Now he has shown his true colours and I believe he has gone completely mad. I fear for the lives of my wife and child and I need help to get them out."

"Which is why you became an informant for us?" prodded Fross as he studied the man in front of him. The changeling gave a quick nod and wrung his hands.

"I know there are some in your house who are some of the best warriors on this side of the mountains, so I came to your man," he gestured at Alaistair, "and began to give him slips of information about my owner and other things. Please, I need your help. I wouldn't show myself if I wasn't serious."

Fross looked at Alaistair with a look that said *Well?* Alaistair shrugged his enormous shoulders in a gesture that meant *Yes*. Fross met the changeling's gray eyes with his mismatched ones and gave him a warm smile.

"Yes, we will help you," Fross said to the man in front of him.

The changeling grinned, relieved.

"I will come back tomorrow and then we can plan."

With that, the changeling quickly disappeared into the hall. Alaistair crashed back onto the couch.

"You didn't let me threaten him," the giant complained.

"Oh? And how were you going to threaten him?" queried Fross, raising an eyebrow at his friend.

"'If you betray us, I'll kill you,'" stated his friend in a menacing voice.

"That sounds silly," teased Fross, crashing beside the giant on the couch, who shrugged in response.

"I read it in a book somewhere, I thought it sounded cool," he responded. There was a tired silence when Alaistair got up and stretched, groaning.

"We should get some rest," he said. "The guards can take care of the perimeter."

Fross cocked an eyebrow. "Whose bed are you going to?" he asked cautiously, his newfound purpose in the Creator making him worry about the sanctity of his own house.

Alaistair grinned. "Mine, but if you hear Paola's little squeal, don't concern yourself with it." And he sauntered off with a small, velvet box appearing in his hand.

Fross shook his head at his friend's retreating figure. "Be careful," he warned him. Fross had known that the two of them had been seeing each other in secret for at least the last fifty years, but he never thought that something would come of it. When you lived unchanging for over 200 years, curse or not, life got boring and monotonous. He walked up the steps to his floor and glanced over to the room where Ash was sleeping. He walked over and put his hand on the door handle. *She is probably tired and I should just let her sleep*, he thought. After listening for a few moments and hearing no screams of terror from Ash, Fross went to his room satisfied and extremely tired.

He was abruptly awakened a few hours later when Paola ran into his room.

"Fross!" she yelled. "Ash is gone!"

His heart stopped as he struggled to understand his friend's words. *Ash is gone! How?*

******

Ash woke up with a cold knife blade at her throat, which was more terrifying than she could have ever thought. She saw green eyes and a pale smile.

"So you have woken up, finally," said Verd, holding the knife to her throat. "I have great plans for you, my love."

Ash clenched her jaw painfully, determined to get away from the knife and from the snake of a man who held it. He began to laugh at the look on her face, a silky laugh that became oily the longer one listened to it.

"You don't want to make an enemy out of me," she said, her words weak and failing to convey her wrath.

He tsked.

"Ah, poor, poor Ash. How do you think you would get out of here?" He mocked her. "You would find it nearly impossible to get out of the house and, if you did," he paused for dramatic effect, "let's just say you would rather stay here."

Ash turned her head away, unwilling to cry in front of the man.

"Whatever you do, and whatever you force me to do," she began, "I will die before bowing to your command, snake."

A throaty laugh erupted from the man.

"Your insults need much sharpening before they sting," he said, taking the knife away from her throat. "But what makes you think I would need you to bow to my command?"

Verd walked out of the room, locking the door on his way out. He made his way up the stairs to a shadowy corner on the ground floor.

"She's awake and is in health," he said to the figure in the shade, "and the spy was sent back with his pay."

"Good," said the figure, unmoving from its position. "Soon the Arcop boy will fall and, when he does, the girl is yours to do what you want with."

Verd bowed. "Your word is law, Master." When he rose from the bow, the figure was gone and Verd shuddered. *Ash, now you and I can be together.*

YUANFEN

Ash spat as the door closed behind the man. She was stuck in a windowless room and the only way in or out was through that door. She moved away from the bed and checked the walls and the floor for hidden cracks but only felt a damp cold coming from the bricks. *I must be underground*, she deduced, and went to study the door. It was wooden and reinforced by metal strips, with no handle on her side of it. She saw no bolts, meaning the door would swing in; that wretched door was for keeping people in and not for keeping others out. Ash's breathing became shallow and erratic, her lungs were feeling crushed as if under a ton of pressure, and the walls seemed closer than before. Ash ran to a wall and crouched down, holding her head in her hands with her eyes closed, trying to focus only on her breathing. *I'm trapped.* The thought swam through her mind over and over as her heart pounded in rhythm with her breathing.

She didn't know how long she crouched there but, after a while, her breathing returned to normal and the terrifying thoughts of being stuck in her room regressed. A hand tapped her shoulder and she jerked away with her eyes closed, fearing the worst.

"Don't worry," a rough-but-soothing voice said. "It is just Eccents and me. We won't hurt you, dear. The master isn't here."

Ash looked up and was greeted with a pair of dancing brown eyes that belonged to an old and craggy face that looked like it had endured many hardships and was framed by white, short hair. Behind the old lady was a younger one, with smart hazel eyes sunken in their sockets and set in an anguished face full of fear and misery. Her long, coiled, and seemingly-brown hair looked like it hadn't been washed in weeks. Ash smiled at her, but Eccents dropped her gaze to the stone floor.

"What a lovely smile you have; it is easy to see why Master wanted you," the old lady said. Ash turned and stared at her in surprise.

"Do you know what he is going to do to me?" Ash asked in a hushed voice. The old lady shook her head, sighing slightly.

"Whatever he plans for your future, let me give you one small piece of advice." The lady leaned closer to Ash. "It would be better to run and die than to try to fight him. He always wins."

Ash shook her head vehemently.

"He is mortal and not a god. He will not win in the end," she said.

The old lady smiled sadly and patted her head.

"Such a beautiful spirit, but you too will be broken. Don't cling to hope for someone to come, they never do." And with that, the two ladies shuffled out of the cell. As they left, Ash noticed the chains that connected their ankles to each others' and the shackles on their wrists. *Slaves.* They closed the door behind them with a thud and Ash was once again alone.

She looked up at the ceiling, her hopeless situation seeming to drown her. The slave-lady's words echoed in her head: *You too will be broken, they never come.* Ash shook her head, not letting herself dwell on what the lady said. She turned her gaze back up to the ceiling.

"Creator, if you are listening . . . " she paused, guilt growing in her. "No, I know you are listening. Please help me through this time. It doesn't look to be easy or fun, but I know you are in control and that your plan is perfect. I don't understand what may come to pass, but please give me the strength and wisdom to stay faithful to you."

Ash began to feel a sense of peace and calmness run through her veins. She smiled and knew what she had to do next: Wait.

The door flew open and in stalked an angry Verd.

"What did those slugs say to you?!" he yelled, his face changing to an ugly beet-red colour.

"Nothing much," replied Ash honestly. "Just that you were going to break my spirit and there was nothing I could do about it."

He smiled a mirthless smile.

"Should have come up with a better lie than that, my love," he purred, stalking over to her. "What did they tell you? Or do I have to invade your memory?"

"You wouldn't dare," Ash whispered in terror.

"Watch me." He smirked and took hold of her chin, gazing deep into her eyes, while his own swirled like scummy green pools.

Ash's head started to ache. She winced, but Verd didn't move. She felt an oily fog come to rest over her brain, making it hard to think. *He won't stop until he knows*, her brain yelled at her, and his mouth twitched into a smile.

"Listen to your brain, my love," he said as he began to pull away. "You know it is right."

He dropped her chin and took a few steps back.

"Well, I do believe I'm needed elsewhere. Thank you for sharing." He walked to the door but turned around at the last moment, looking at Ash, who had slumped to the floor in exhaustion from her mental fight. "And if you keep up with the Creator nonsense, I'll make sure Lord Fross pays dearly for it. No one and nothing will stop me."

He turned and disappeared into the darkness outside the room, the door slamming shut.

"Please keep Fross safe," Ash breathed into the air, knowing that only the Creator could keep him safe.

******

Fross looked at the bedsheets. They were messed, like someone had slept in them but not for long. *Why hadn't she put up a fight?* he wondered, as his heart seemed to crash within itself. Ash was the most stubborn woman he had ever known, feistier than a pack of wild foxes. The only reason imaginable to explain this was that she had left willingly.

His heart crumbled and he fell to his knees, crying out internally that he had loved someone who had been working against him all this time. He sat there for a while, tears slowly creeping down his face, until he heard the light footsteps of Paola and the significantly heavier ones of Alaistair. They walked into the room and sat on either side of their heartbroken boss. As they sat there in silence, Fross remembered something that Ash had said just a few days before, when they had been in the garden. It had been about love. Fross closed his eyes and tried to pull up the memory.

She had been glowing in the sun and Fross had asked her a stupid question about how one would define love. She turned to him, smiling and said:

"Love is patient and kind. It is not jealous, nor does it brag. It isn't proud and it doesn't dishonour others. It is not self-seeking nor easily angered and it keeps no record of wrongs. Love does not enjoy evil things but rejoices in truth and justice. It always protects, trusts, and hopes. It is forever enduring and love never fails. It doesn't matter what type of love you are talking about—whether with your friends, parents, or wife, those aspects are shown in all types of love."

Fross snapped back to the present and saw Paola pick up a glass cup that Fross hadn't noticed before.

"What's that doing here?" he murmured, taking the cup into his own hands.

"Ash was given it by Noah Pridegazer before she went to bed," replied Paola sadly. "I'll take it down to the healers to check for any suspicious potions. With all that has happened, I just want to double-check."

As the she-elf left, Fross noticed a small, practical ring with a square diamond in it.

"I guess she said 'yes'?" he asked his friend with a smile. Alaistair grinned back.

"Yes, it was the most terrifying experience of my life, waiting for her response." He turned serious as Fross's eyes dropped to back to the bed. "You love her, don't you?" Alaistair asked gently.

Fross turned to the giant. "Was I that obvious?"

The giant nodded. "Almost as obvious as her blatant love for you."

Hearing those words, Fross's heart healed as quickly as it had broken.

"Don't think for a second that Ash is behind this," Alaistair said. "I would die before I let someone get between you two."

ANAGAPESIS

"What is happening down here?" Haon asked Blanche, who was looking at the small glass cup that Paola had found.

"Checking the cup for any sign of a sleeping potion," replied the lady in her husky voice.

Haon watched her for a few minutes and jumped when he heard a voice from the other room.

"Blanche!" Chester called. "Could you give me a hand with these vials?"

Blanche quickly excused herself and went to the other room. Haon moved quickly, changing the cup with an exact copy from the kitchen and hiding the original in his bag. Blanche returned and Haon said his farewell and returned to the meeting room where Vincent had asked him to meet.

Haon smiled to himself as he walked through the castle. He'd slipped in the potion right before his brother had taken it up from the kitchen to Ash in an act of goodwill. Unfortunately for his twin, this little act of kindness would end his career, and maybe his life, if luck was with Haon. He sighed. Since they had been born, Noah had always been the better brother. After over 200 years, Haon was sick of it and had devised his own sly plans. If some other people got hurt, so be it, but if his brother took the fall, it was ultimately worth it.

He looked at his watch and growled. He would be late for his meeting with Vincent, which would then most likely then make him late to meet Verd, on whose bad side Haon would rather not be.

* * * * * *

Ash was bored. She had been in this cell all day and she was bored. She rolled onto her bed, hoping to sleep to pass the time. Suddenly, there was a screech and then a clank as the door opened. In walked two guards, dressed completely in green garb and with masks covering their faces. She sat up, surprised and happy that there was at least some change to the scenery.

"Come with us," one said, grabbing Ash's shirt.

Ash walked to the door, knowing the other option was to be dragged, which would reduce her strength. The two guards took her through winding passages, always going up. They finally passed a ground-floor window, which proved Ash's suspicions of having been underground. They soon stopped in front of a black door, which one of the guards banged on. The door opened a crack and out peeked a small, frowning face with dull green eyes and a shock of red hair. Seeing Ash, the eyes sparked to life and the door opened to completely, letting in the trio.

Ash looked around and saw what looked like the healers' room at Fross's place, except it was bigger and with more sinister-looking tools. A lady with silver hair popped out from behind a machine and nodded to a table.

"Strap her down there," the lady ordered, and the guards did as they were told.

Ash struggled, not liking the idea of being strapped to anything. However, the guards were too strong and they easily overpowered her, leaving her tired from trying.

A door opened and in walked Verd and another man, who Verd kept referring to as "Professor." The two of them came close to Ash and studied her. As Verd looked at the young lady named Ash, he thought he saw the story of an entire civilization running through her veins and written on her skin. He looked at the balding professor and said, "You know what to do." He walked out of the room, the door swinging shut behind him with a resounding clank.

The old man smiled creepily at Ash and turned to a tray of all sorts of painful-looking extraction tools. Ash saw the tools and stared elsewhere, not wanting to think about what was going to happen to her. The lady was also busy treating some cloth with an odd yellow mixture that smelled putrid. She turned and smiled, seeing Ash watching her.

"Night, night," she said, and covered Ash's face with the cloth. Ash blacked out immediately.

******

Verd was pacing the room as he waited, the tension seeming to increase as every minute passed. When he was about to return to the surgery room, the professor came in.

"Well?" Verd asked impatiently.

"She is a match, congratulations," said the man, grinning.

Verd returned the smile. "On to phase two, Professor Crow."

******

Ash awoke and for a second thought she was back at Arcop Manor, but that was shattered when she realized that she was tied to the bed. She began to struggle, and the old slave appeared.

"Let me help you," she said, and cut the ropes. "My name is Typics," she said when she was finished. "Eccents and I are going to help prepare you for tonight."

"Tonight?" asked Ash in a hoarse voice. Her throat was drier than the raging wastelands to the east.

Eccents came into view with a cup of water that Ash drank greedily.

"Thank you," she said to the girl, and turned her attention back to Typics. "What is happening tonight?"

The old slave looked around fearfully and then down at her clasped hands. Ash followed with her own gaze and gasped at what she saw. The slave's smallest finger had been recently cut off but there was no bandage to prevent infection.

"You are going to be married to the master," the slave responded, ignoring the noise that Ash made at having seen her disfigurement.

Ash looked past the two ladies in horror and saw a black wedding dress that looked like cobwebs. *Oh, Creator help me*, she prayed silently, knowing that she was but a slave to the whims of the hateful man, Verd.

* * * * * *

The meeting with Vincent had had more than just a few guards; the warriors and Fross had been there too. Haon had been fine, sitting there and answering the questions regarding where he had been the night before and so on. However, when he had gotten up to leave, his bag had hit the table's edge with a resounding clinking noise. The master asked him to remove the bag and Haon knew he was caught.

A few minutes later, he was in the dungeon, being interrogated more thoroughly by the elf and the mage while the giant and master, along with the newcomer, watched.

"It seems we have found the mole in our walls," the mage mused, a dangerous glint gleaming in his eye.

"Where is Ash?" the she-elf asked again, but Haon wouldn't respond.

The warrior looked at the mage and nodded. Haon began to sweat as the mage came forward. Though Kogu was the head of the castle's defence, he was also a powerful mind reader and could send commands to one's brain that would be worse than torture.

"I won't ever tell you," Haon spat.

The mage grinned a wild grin. "Well, you don't have much of a choice in the matter."

******

It had taken half an hour to get the information from the traitor. It was time they didn't have, and now Fross was beside himself as he and the three warriors suited up for battle.

"I'll have Vincent take us to the center of Fallowbloom Retreat and wait there for five minutes until we are in place. We have to stop the wedding before it is too late," ordered Fross, his voice cracking at the end.

The warriors nodded solemnly. This was no time for fun and games; this was time for death. Fross had said their main goal was to bring out Ash alive and unharmed. Paola looked at Alaistair, worried.

"Don't do something rash," she squeezed her fiancé's hand.

"I serve Fross as do you," he reminded her, "but I will do my best." He kissed her on the lips, the first time that they had shown public affection to each other, and held her hand for a second longer. "I love you, always will," he murmured. Looking into her eyes, he knew the feeling was mutual.

There was a small coughing sound and the fiancés turned, weapons at the ready. Syn materialized and Alaistair relaxed.

"Are you ready?" he asked the changeling, who nodded solemnly, eyes flashing their reptilian green as fury seemed to roll through the giant.

"He has had his last day of enslaving others. We'd best act quickly. He has already taken a digit from one of his human slaves and he says my Phase is next," the changeling said. "The wedding is happening at sundown."

Fross, who had joined the group, nodded and checked the sun.

"Let's go. We have about an hour to get there." He looked at Syn. "Do you know the shortest way there?"

Syn nodded and went to the car, taking point on the trip.

Paola looked at the changeling's retreating form and then looked at her fiancé.

"When did you meet him?" she asked him.

"I'll tell you after. It is a complicated story," Alaistair replied as they entered the second car.

Cathect

Ash looked at her reflection in the mirror and shuddered. She looked like a lifeless doll in the black dress. When the slaves began to come at her with makeup, she backed away.

"Don't put that on me, please," she begged, but the slaves shook their heads and Ash knew there wasn't a choice to be made. It was going on.

She closed her eyes and sat back in the chair as she felt them spread creams and brushes over her face. When they were done, she looked back in the mirror and saw a pale mask of false beauty. She closed her eyes again, trying not to cry, knowing that crying would only make her have to get it redone, which would cause Verd's anger to erupt. Nevertheless, she couldn't stop the one tear that crept down her face.

A door opened and she heard footsteps, some leaving and then a lone pair approaching her.

"I see you are ready, my love," Verd purred into her ear.

Ash opened her eyes and saw him staring at her as she looked in the mirror. He grabbed both her hands with one of his and tied them with a black ribbon.

"Couldn't let you play hard to get," he said, smelling her hair, which was all piled up on top of her head.

"If my hands were free, you would no longer be alive," she snarled. "Unlike what Dasica says, in my culture kidnapping is a killing offence."

"Don't shove your ridiculous ideas into my face," he hissed, slapping her cheek.

She winced but met his seething gaze with her own fiery one. He laughed a rough laugh.

"You will be fun to break, but, for now, we should get to our wedding, my love." He pulled her to her feet and grabbed her bound wrists and dragged Ash behind him.

Ash looked for a weapon as they rushed down the corridor, but found none. Verd stopped in front of a pair of double doors that reminded Ash of her father's throne room. He pushed them open, dropping her hands. She remembered her hairpins and reached up to grab one but Verd turned before she could get to one. He dusted off his green suit and took her wrists as they walked at a more leisurely pace to where a man and a lady in military garb stood.

This is it, Ash thought as tears streamed down her face. She stopped walking, causing Verd to stop and look at her in annoyance.

"Prysm!" he yelled. The woman who was dressed like a general walked over. "Take her the rest of the way."

The lady nodded and hoisted Ash over her shoulder and walked behind Verd, to where the man was waiting. Ash saw a small dagger in the lady's belt and grabbed it, hiding it by her wrist. When Prysm dropped her by Verd, Ash snuck the blade into her bust. Verd grabbed her hands and turned to the man who looked like he would fall dead at any moment, due to his ancient and sickly-looking figure. In the corner of her eye, she thought she saw a small shadow creeping closer to the small wedding ceremony. Ash closed her eyes as tears began to fall down her cheeks. *Oh Creator, please help me.*

The sickly man began, in a weak voice, the traditional wedding ceremony, as Ash's heart pounded in fear.

"Why are you doing this?" whispered Ash to Verd. She strained to hear anything that could be the sounds of a rescue but there was nothing but the droning of the man. "What have I done to you that makes you want this match?"

"Why am I doing this?" asked Verd, indignantly. "Your father had first arranged for you to marry me as part of a deal that was very expensive for me. Then, in swept in that filthy Fross, who took both your hand and the deal that was meant for me. Now I can take back what is rightfully mine."

"I will never be yours," Ash spat back.

Verd chuckled. "You already are."

The sickly man finished saying the last sentence of the traditional ceremony.

"You may now kiss the bride."

Verd planted a quick kiss on Ash and grinned evilly.

Soon the ceremony was done and Verd dragged her to a bedroom on the highest floor.

He threw her on the floor and closed the door while she regained her breath. Ash saw him come close to her and crawled away as best she could in the encumbering boat of a dress. He grabbed her dress and pulled her back, drawing out his blade in the process. She screamed and tried to get away but was trapped.

He shook his head.

"What a pity . . . "

"Let me go!" Ash begged, even though she knew it would do no good. "Please," she sobbed, "please."

"You could have been queen if you had accepted my advances. It's a pity you chose this path instead—" Verd lifted his dagger and brought it down, tearing through her dress and scraping her leg slightly. "—to be a slave," he said, as he lifted the blade again to cut the dress away from her.

Ash kicked him as she tried to roll away from his grasp. The material, caught in Verd's hand, ripped and Ash was left with a ragged skirt and bodice. Verd smiled wildly as he stalked toward her like a predator intent on his prey.

* * * * * *

Fross's heart was pounding with terror as he ran through the Fallowbloom Retreat. They had dispatched all of the few guards there, and the general, but there was no sign of Verd or Ash. He threw open the doors to the throne room and saw an old man lying on the floor with a small woman beside him. He ran over to them and saw that with the man had taken a knife to the stomach. He was still in the process of dying, though the woman was trying in vain to save him. *I'm too late!* Fross thought as he bent down to see the man.

"Where did they go?" he seethed, as the man's eyes fixed on him. The woman pointed to the staircase he'd passed on his way in.

"Last floor, gold door," the man choked out before dying.

The almond-skinned woman looked up, her violet eyes flashing a reptilian green as her golden hair, soaked with the man's blood, fell out of its ponytail.

"Go!" she yelled at him.

Fross, with no time to waste, ran to the stairs, going up two and three at a time. When he had made it to the top and had begun to search for the gold door as the man had said, he heard a bone-chilling scream and ran in that direction, knowing it was Ash's voice and fearing the worst.

* * * * * *

Alaistair saw his friend run frantically up the stairs and began to follow him, but hesitated to wonder if he should bring the others. He heard a scream and decided to go, praying that the others would find them.

* * * * * *

Ash was cornered and her hands were still bound up in the ribbon, though it had loosened slightly. She grabbed the knife from her bust and held it out in front of her, trying to ward off Verd. He chuckled and she felt searing pain run through her mind. She screamed, dropping the knife, and held her head, tears running down her face. She looked up to see Verd holding a small crystal ball that disappeared into his pocket as he walked over. He crouched in front of her and the pain in her head began to lessen.

"Don't think about picking up that blade or your head will feel like it is being crushed again," the man warned her.

Ash dug her fingers into her hair and felt a metal object. It was a hairpin. She made a mad dash past the vicious man, who made an animalistic noise as he turned to her. Ash smiled the type of smile that would make most people stay away from her, but Verd wasn't in his right mind. He stalked closer and she pulled out more hairpins, dropping them to the floor and letting her hair fall down her shoulders, concealing the last hairpin. He smiled a sick smile.

"I knew you would make the right decision in the end," he purred as he walked over and stopped right in front of her. He tilted up her chin and gave her a look that said everything was in his control.

Ash grasped the pin and stabbed him in the chest. He paused and looked down at the pin, pulling it out.

"Bad move," he seethed. "You just awoke an indestructible beast."

Ash's heart plummeted as he struck her with his hand. She flew across the room, landing just shy of the bed. He was there in an instant and picked her up by her neck, tossing her onto the bed. He had ripped off most of her skirt when there was a shout.

"Get away from my bride!" Fross leapt into the room, his lethal, but beautiful, longsword with a light glow was out and ready to do battle.

Ash scurried away from Verd as he turned away from her to fight.

"Ah, so you were the one she was promised to," the man said, turning to Fross. "I'll make you regret that decision."

A blade with a fell light materialized in the man's hands and, with that, the two of them charged at each other. The sounds of weapons clashing reverberated throughout the house. The two of them, locked in battle, moved swiftly and deadly, each looking for an opening in the other's defence. Fross found one and stabbed Verd in the stomach. He smiled terribly, pulled himself off of the sword, and resumed fighting.

"I cannot be killed!" he roared victoriously as he took down Fross's defence.

Ash looked around for a weapon as she heard Fross groan. She turned to see that he had been slashed across the chest. Blood seeped from the wound, as it did from others on his body.

Ash acted without thought. She jumped onto Verd's back and yanked him back from the death blow he was about to inflict on her betrothed. She plunged a hand into his pocket, looking for the crystal ball and knowing it had something to do with his sudden invincibility. She grabbed it just as he flung her off of him.

"You should know better than to side with the losers," he hissed at her, slashing her thigh.

She screamed in agony but held on to the crystal ball, hiding it from his sight. *Destroy it!* her mind screamed at her. Verd turned back to Fross and raised his sword above his head with both hands. *Crush it!* There was an inhuman roar of rage that sounded as a giant, golden blur appeared and covered Fross. Ash blinked and saw Alaistair on top of Fross, with his sword up to block Verd's blow. The powerful blade, stronger than Alaistair's, sliced through it and quickly cut through the giant's chest. The giant continued and tackled Verd to the ground, taking out his dagger and stabbing Verd in the side. Verd retaliated by knocking Alaistair in the head and, while he was dazed, picked him up by the throat and ran his sword through the giant, letting the giant's body fall, limp.

Ash screamed in horrific agony as she saw her friend fall upon Fross. Triumphantly, Verd turned toward her just as Ash smashed the crystal ball into pieces on the dark floor. He stopped in the middle of taking a step and looked down to see blood darkening his clothes where he had been wounded by both Fross and Ash.

He fell to the ground, gasping for breath. As Ash walked over to him, he begged, "Finish me now, don't let me linger."

Ash levelled a stare at him and pointed to where Alaistair and Fross were.

"Those are my friends," her voice cracked. "You lost all hope of mercy from me when you attacked them." She squatted down, shook her head, and frowned. "I pray you never take a breath without remembering the breaths you've taken away."

Ash ran over to where Fross was laying on his back, having gotten out from under the giant. Ash knelt before her friend and checked his pulse. It was there but weakening fast.

"We have to get him to a hospital, fast," Ash said, but Fross shook his head.

"It is too late for that," he said, tears filling his eyes.

Alaistair groaned and moved his hand to hold Ash's, looking her in the eye.

"I believe," he wheezed out. "The Creator wants me to come to Him now."

Ash nodded, tears filling her eyes. There were footsteps and then a gasp. Paola knelt before her fiancé as Ash moved to be beside Fross.

"No! No! No, mi amor, not like this!" the elf cried as she saw the damage. She bent lower to hear what the giant was saying and then whispered something back to him. Alaistair smiled and turned his head to Fross.

"Take care of them," he begged, and Fross nodded.

"You have my word."

Kogu rushed in and knelt before Alaistair, his amber eyes glowing as he tried to heal the gash on his chest. Alaistair shook his head slightly.

"Remember our deal," he said, and Kogu nodded his head in reverence.

Paola turned her wet violet eyes, which were made more heartbreakingly brilliant by crying, to Ash, who was holding her friend's hand. Paola combed back Alaistair's hair, her gaze never leaving his face until his golden eyes became dull and his spirit was swept away. The elf rested her head on her love's shoulder and wept light-violet tears, as if her irises themselves had abandoned her eyes. Everyone was silent and the only thing to be heard was the heartbroken wails of the little elf. Fross, with help of Kogu's healing powers, closed his friend's eyes and stood, not bothering to hide his tears from his warriors and soldiers. Ash stood beside him, holding his hand.

"Tonight," he began, once Paola's wails had diminished to silent sobs, "we have lost a good man who, in his final hours, became a great man, sacrificing all to become a servant of the Creator and my brother. He died to save us, like Joshua did so many millennia ago, and his memory will always be with us."

There was the shuffle of feet as Fross's guards came to lift the giant's body. Ash went to help Paola, who then clung to her desperately, saying nothing. A guard—Ash thought her name was Onul—came over to her.

"What do you want to be done with him?" she asked, gesturing to Verd's still body.

"Throw him out onto the ground, to rot," said Ash, who then walked with Paola, following Alaistair's still body.

Redamancy

The summer showers began that night and continued into the morning.

The funeral was held out in the rain, the skies crying at the loss of the giant. Ash held an umbrella above her and Paola, holding her fragile friend close to her chest as the tears rolled down the little elf's face. Ash listened to the man who was presiding over the funeral. He was another servant of the Creator, who talked about the importance of true love and sacrifice.

Soon the funeral was over and there was a fire set for Alaistair in the crypt of his burial. Paola and Ash sat in quiet reverence in front of the crypt for a few minutes. Finally, Paola spoke.

"I should have been there sooner," wept Paola. "I just couldn't make it in time."

"What are you saying, Paola?" asked Ash, worry clouding her eyes.

Paola turned her clear eyes to her friend.

"I'm pregnant," she admitted, tears rolling down her cheeks. "And now Alaistair is gone."

"It is his?" asked Ash, eyes widening in surprise.

The elf nodded and placed her hands on her stomach.

"What am I going to do?"

"You are going to stay here with us," Ash said, placing a hand on Paola's small shoulder. "I'm not leaving you to fend for yourself."

"But I'm worthless!" cried Paola.

"No, you aren't!" cried Ash. "Not to me, or Fross, or anyone here. Please, stay."

Paola finally agreed and Ash sighed, knowing that there would be more conversations like this in the future.

* * * * * *

Six months had passed since the death of Alaistair. Ash spent most of her time with either Paola or Fross, and sometimes with Kogu, consoling them about their longtime friend. Verd's changelings had stayed, too, after lots of encouragement from Fross. Phase had given birth to a healthy boy, Westcott "Ringer" Gloryoak, who was the happiest and the most spoiled child in all of Dasica, with shining brown eyes and dark golden hair that made all the staff coo over him. Verd's two slaves were also brought to Arcop Manor, but Typics succumbed to her wounds a few days after arriving. Eccents survived, became a willing part of the household, and renamed herself Jessica Connor. She trained under Annabella Tyler, the housekeeper, to become a lady's maid. Verd's guards, who had been knocked out at the Fallowbloom Retreat, had disappeared without a trace and his mansion had burned down to the ground, leaving no evidence behind.

One day, Ash woke up to a letter that asked her to come out to the pavilion in the large garden. The sky was heavy with snow. She slipped on a creamy shawl and walked to the small structure. Fross was there waiting for her.

Ash smiled and was happy to see it returned on his own face. There were days that he would seem to drift away from reality and into grief, as did the elf, who had only surfaced from her own grief a month before, when the baby she was carrying really began to show.

"So, why was I brought out here?" she asked Fross, who had turned sombre at her question.

"Well, my reason is two-fold. First, I want to tell you something. I have wanted to for a while now, but I am a coward sometimes," he began. Ash gestured for him to continue, though worry began to seep into her mind. "You know that I've been alive for over two centuries, but what you don't know is my original name." He took a big breath and stared deeply into her eyes as he continued. "My original name is Pyatro Forester Archer II."

Ash put her scarred hand on Fross's shoulder.

"Fross," she began, "I don't care what name was your given name, or whether you go by it or not. I am happy that you shared this with me. You are the man I fell in love with, regardless of what name you use, and, to me, you are no coward."

Fross grinned as he pulled her close to give her a kiss on her head.

"Well, then, this marks a special occasion," he murmured into her hair as he hugged her.

"What is the special occasion?" she asked Fross, who grinned.

"Oh, just wanted to spend some time with the most beautiful lady in the entire castle," he said, taking her hand.

Ash turned, pulling her hand out of his grasp when she saw roses and lit candles.

"What is all of this?" she asked, turning back to Fross, who was kneeling.

"Take my hand," he said, reaching out with his hand.

"Why?"

His cheeks deepened into a rosy red.

"I'm trying to ask you to marry me again. The right way this time. So, please, take my hand," he explained, sounding exasperated.

She gave him her hand and he slipped a ruby-and-diamond ring onto her finger.

"Ash Cartier," he began, "would you do me the honour of becoming my wife?"

Ash smiled, tears rolling down her face.

"Yes!"

Fross jumped up, swung her around, and placed her outside the pavilion.

"I will find who killed your parents," he promised. His voice deepened. "I love you, Ash."

"I love you too, Fross," Ash replied, putting her arms around his neck.

They sealed their declarations of love with a kiss.

Thank you, Creator, for giving me this man, Ash prayed as the two of them broke their kiss to see snow falling around them.

CHARACTER DESCRIPTION SHEET

Cartier Clan

1) Ash Cartier [Ash Cart-E-eh] – Shadowwalker, daughter to Marie and Lucas Cartier, heir to Cartier Castle. *(Brown shaggy hair in a double-layered braid, blue eyes, strong oval face, ivory skin, curvy frame but quite muscular, 5'11", human.)*

2) Marie (Etton) Cartier [Mar-y (é-tt-on) Cart-E-eh] – Mother to Ash Cartier and husband to Lucas Cartier. *(Silver shaggy hair, brown eyes, porcelain skin, small round face, athletic frame, 5'6", human.)*

3) Lucas Cartier [Lu-cas Cart-E-eh] – Father to Ash Cartier and husband to Marie Cartier, head elder of Cartier Castle. *(Silver, oily hair; blue eyes; warm, beige skin; long face; burn scar on left side of his forehead, which runs to his left nostril; slight frame; 5'10"; human.)*

4) Carmel Baum [Car-mel B*omb*] – Trainer to Ash Cartier and Gilith Preslar in all studies outside of the house. *(Silver hair in a double-layered braid, red eyes, golden skin, square face, red tribal marks on cheekbones [two lines stacked on top of each other], muscular frame, 5'9", human, unknown tribe.)*

5) Gilith Preslar [Gill-ith Press-lar] – Childhood friend to Ash Cartier. *(Blond curly hair, amber eyes, coffee-coloured skin, round face, stubble on chin and jaw, wiry frame, 6'0". Half-mage and half-human [abomination].)*

6) Adam Firedraft [Adam Fire-draft) – Second elder and councillor to Lucas Cartier. *(Chestnut dreadlocks, brown eyes, almond-coloured skin, thin face, scrawny frame, 5'10", human.)*

Arcop Clan

1) Fross Arcop [Fross Argh-cop] – Slayer, Lord of Arcop Manor. *(Long, dark-brown hair; one dark-brown eye and one forest-green eye; caramel skin; mole just above the right side of his mouth; slender, but muscular, frame; 6'0"; human.)*

2) Vincent Forestbreak [Vincent Forest-break] – Head of Arcop guards. *(Ginger-coloured dreadlocks; glue eyes; espresso-coloured skin; boney, warm face; lion's-paw tattoo on right side of his right eyebrow; athletic frame; 5'8"; human.)*

3) Rifiky Haddani [Rif-E-ky Had-any] – Arcop guard. *(Short, silver hair; amber eyes; porcelain skin; strong face; freckles on cheeks and forehead; big frame; 6'1"; Mage.)*

4) Noah Pridegazer [Noah Pride-gazer] – Brother to Haon Pridegazer, an Arcop guard. *(Green hair, pink eyes, fawn-coloured skin, strong face, green goatee, brawny frame, 5'4", Elf.)*

5) Haon Pridegazer [Ha-own Pride-gazer] – Brother to Noah Pridegazer, an Arcop guard. *(Light-green, wavy hair; pink eyes; autumnal skin; long face; subtle frame; 5'4"; Elf.)*

6) Vala Sternhelm [Vah-lah Stern-helm] – Arcop guard. *(White, oily hair; brown eyes; suntanned skin; boney face; freckles on cheeks and forehead; delicate frame; 6'1"; human.)*

7) Onul Jebel [On-ule Jeb-bell] – Arcop guard. *(Red hair, green eyes, ivory skin, boney face, skinny frame, 5'7", human.)*

8) Alaistair Reh [Al-i-stare Ray] – General of Arcop Manor, best friend to Fross. *(Golden hair; golden eyes; smooth, maple-coloured skin; half-feral face; lean frame; 6'5"; unknown classification.)*

9) Kogu Masu [Ko-goo Mass-ew] – Offensive coordinator of Arcop Manor, Fross's friend. *(Short, silver hair; amber eyes; honey-bronze skin; full, menacing face; fragile frame; 6'3"; Mage.)*

10) Paola Lambert [Pa-o-la Lamb-bert] – Defensive coordinator of Arcop Manor, Fross's friend. *(Light-green, wavy hair; violet eyes; warm, silky skin; cheerful face; slim frame; 5'2"; Elf.)*

11) Annabella Tyler – Arcop housekeeper. *(Brown hair, hazel eyes, teak wood-coloured skin; thin face; delicate frame; 5'5"; Human.)*

12) Richard Tucket [Richard Tuck-et] – Arcop chef. *(Black hair, sea-green eyes, riviera skin, friendly face, moles on his neck, thick frame, 5'11", human.)*

13) Chester Ward – Arcop in-house healer. *(Blonde hair in a ponytail; bulging, hazel eyes; chestnut-coloured skin; strong, lively face; large beard; slim frame; 5'6"; human.)*

14) Blanche Todd [Blahn-sh Todd] – Assistant Arcop healer. *(Pink hair in a bun, violet eyes, bisque skin, radiant face, big frame, 5'10", unknown classification)*

15) Laura Piper – Arcop engineer. *(Blonde, curly hair; clear blue eyes; beige skin; chiseled, innocent face; freckles on cheeks; strong frame; 5'0"; human.)*

Winfield Clan

1) Verd Winfield [Ver-d Win-field] – Master of Fallowbloom Retreat. *(Brown, curly hair; hooded green eyes; soft, sand-coloured skin; strong, feral face; narrow frame; 6'0"; human.)*

2) Prysm Wright [Prism Right] – General of Fallowbloom Retreat. *(Purple hair; bloodshot, silver eyes; porcelain skin; angular face; broad frame; 5'9"; abomination.)*

3) Lucifer Zayne – Verd Winfield's right-hand man. *(Blond hair, hazel eyes, golden skin, craggy face, light frame, 5'11", human.)*

4) Prof. Crow – Head Scientist. *(Silver hair; bloodshot, hazel eyes; espresso-coloured skin; weary face; scrawny frame; 5'7"; human genius.)*

5) Dr. Daisy – Scientist/healer. *(Coiled, silver hair; green eyes; ivory skin; chiseled face; thin frame; 5'5"; human.)*

6) Grime – Scientists' peon. *(Red hair; small, hazel eyes; chestnut skin; lean, frowning face; lean frame; 5'0"; human.)*

7) Syn [sin] – Spy, husband of Phase. *(Black, curly hair; grey eyes; soft, honey-coloured skin; thin, time-worn face; sturdy frame; 6'0"; changeling.)*

8) Phase – Spy, wife of Syn. *(Golden hair in a ponytail; violet eyes; almond-coloured skin; long, worried face; sturdy frame; 6'1"; changeling.)*

9) Typics [Tip-picks] – Slave. *(Short, white hair; brown eyes; porcelain skin; craggy, worried face; old, fragile frame; 5'8"; human.)*

10) Eccents [Eh-scents] – Slave. *(Brown, coiled hair; deep blue eyes; warm, beige skin; chiseled, anguished face; malnourished, brawny frame; 5'6"; human.)*

Clanless

1) Black Eagle Gang [B.E.G.] – a local gang filled with hatred and wrath against the government and the rich.

2) Master Blackstrike – Overseer.

GLOSSARY

- Ketacept [Ket-ah-cept]: A pain reliever that you ingest. A blue colour.

- Icofoxin Temonadryl [I-co-foz-in Te-mon-ah-dril]: A paste to put on bruises or minor wounds, to aid in speeding up the healing process. White in colour.

- Mirage Couture Boots: Boots made of unusual leather, which are water- and weatherproof. Created by mages.

CPSIA information can be obtained
at www.ICGtesting.com
Printed in the USA
LVHW012234280419
615836LV00002BA/2

9 781612 447346